For The Sake of

For the Sake of Love

For The Sake of Love II

To the extent that the image or images on the cover of this book depict a person or persons, such person or persons are merely models and are not intended to portray any character or characters featured in this book.

This book is a work of fiction. References to historical events, real people, or real places are used fictitiously. Other characters, names, places, and events are products of the author's imagination and any resemblance to actual events or places or persons living, or deceased is entirely coincidental.

Copyright © 2022 by Antoinette R. Davis

All rights reserved. No part of this book may be reproduced in any form without the author's consent whatsoever.

For more information, contact:

www.onefictionqueen.com

While money may not purchase true happiness, it certainly has the power to orchestrate a hidden darkness—like a murder.

Terri always thought she could handle the weight of her family's secrets, but the truth has a way of clawing its way to the surface, especially when it's buried under layers of manipulation and despair. For years, her mother and sister controlled her thoughts, twisting her reality to fit their narrative. Terri, bruised but resilient, began piecing together fragmented memories and unsettling whispers—a puzzle that painted a chilling picture.

As the secrets unravel, they bring with them a series of mysterious deaths that make Terri question everything. Each body that appears feels like a warning, a dark message that someone is desperate to keep buried. The stakes rise, and she realizes that unearthing these truths could cost her more than just her sanity; it could cost her life.

Fueled by a mixture of fear and determination, Terri sets out to confront her past and the forces that seek to silence her. The deeper she digs, the more she uncovers a web of deceit where loyalty is a façade and safety is an illusion. Terri must decide—will she finally reclaim her voice, or will she become just another victim of a relentless cycle of abuse? The clock is ticking, and the shadows are closing in.

Renee is about to turn Terri's big day upside down. With an air of confidence, she strides into the wedding venue, ready to make a statement. The tension in the air is intense as guests turn to see who has disrupted the ceremony.

"Surprise, everyone!" Renee declares, her voice dripping with defiance. "Payback is a bitch, and I'm here to settle the score!"

Kamal, caught in the middle of the brewing storm, feels the weight of the situation. Terri, blindsided by Renee's unexpected appearance, realizes that this confrontation isn't just about her wedding—it's a battle of wills. The stakes are high, and as guests murmur in shock, Renee stands firm, prepared to reveal the truth to everyone present.

As the chaos unfolds, it becomes clear that this day will be remembered for more than just vows—it's a showdown with emotions running wild and the promise of consequences hanging in the balance.

Mess with me but not my children, they opened up hell's door but they didn't expect the devil in red bottom boots.

For The Sake of Love II

Chapter One

A Frenzy

For The Sake of Love II

Terri screams in the phone, "Nina, oh my God!"

"Where are you, Terri? What's happening!"

Terri is frantic, "Someone just hit the car, and it flipped over."

"Where's the baby."

Terri tries to turn her head but can't, "I can't see the baby, and I can't hear him." Terri starts crying

Nina jumps into action, "I'm turning on the locator, calling 911, and I'm on my way to you."

"Don't hang up, I'm scared. Nina."

"Okay, I'll call 911 from my other phone.

In the meantime, someone else has called 911, and bystanders are trying to get Terri and the baby out of the car.

"I hear people banging on the glass and sirens."

"I'm in my car, and the locator gave me your location, so I'll be there in fifteen minutes."

"Nina, hurry; I'm scared, and I can't see the baby."

Nina starts to tear up; she wipes her eyes and drives to Terri.

As the ambulance doors swung open, the paramedics sprang into action, their uniforms catching the pale light of the early morning. The Fire Department's crew followed closely behind, their helmets glinting as they rushed towards the scene. With urgency and precision, they worked together, carefully extracting Terri from

For The Sake of Love II

the twisted wreckage of the car. Moments later, they gently cradled her baby, ensuring both mother and child were safe and secure. The tension in the air began to ease as they managed to free them, their expressions a mix of relief and determination.

Terri hears her baby screaming and then nothing, "My baby," she screams.

"He's not breathing," says the paramedic to the other. They quickly put Baby Gary and Terri inside the ambulance.

Terri stands frozen in place, her heart pounding in her chest as she watches the paramedics rush to her baby. The sterile scent of antiseptic fills the air, mingling with the overwhelming sense of fear that grips her. Bright lights from the ambulance cast harsh shadows, illuminating their focused faces as they expertly maneuvered around her child. One paramedic gently presses a hand on her baby's tiny chest while another prepares equipment, their voices steady and calm, yet tinged with urgency. Terri feels tears stinging her eyes as she tries to absorb the scene—the frantic beeping of machines, the worried expressions, the desperate hope that everything will be alright. "What's wrong,"

"We don't know yet, but as long as he's hooked up to this machine, we can keep him alive," says the paramedic.

Nina arrives as the ambulance is pulling off; she follows the ambulance and calls Kamal on his cell phone. "Kamal, there's been an accident with Terri and the baby, and they rushed them to the hospital.

"What hospital are they going to?"

Nina gives him the address, and he quickly changes out of his scrubs and jumps into his car. It's starting to rain, and Kamal can barely see how to drive.

Nina makes it to the emergency room and asks for Terri, but she's not allowed to go in the back.

Terri has a few bruises and a cut on her forehead; the paramedics bandaged her up, and she's good. However, the baby was thrown from his car seat and is in critical condition.

Terri doesn't have her cell phone, so she can't call anyone; she's sitting alone, waiting for the doctors to tell her something.

Nina reaches out to Terri's Auntie Pam to let her know what is going on; however, she's reluctant to call Terri's mother, Delores.

Nina remembers the last time Terri was in the hospital, and Kamal contacted Delores, but she didn't bother to show up.

Nina decides to call Delores anyway, "Ms. Delores, hi this is Nina, Terri and the baby were in a bad car accident and, and "Nina breaks down crying, "I just thought you would want to know."

Delores is surprisingly upset. "Of course, I want to know. That's my daughter and grandson. Where are they?"

Nina gives Delores the details and then calls Terri's aunt Pam and Terri's Office.

DeeDee walks into the kitchen where Delores sits, "Why are you staring into space like that?

"Your sister and nephew were in a car accident and it's bad."

DeeDee opens the refrigerator and grabs some grapes, "Wow, she can't catch a break."

"Is that all you can say? Where is your heart? Your sister and nephew were in a car accident, and Nina said it's really bad."

DeeDee closes the refrigerator and bites down on a big juicy green grape, "My heart is where it has always been." DeeDee walks out of the kitchen.

In that instant, a chilling truth dawned on Delores—she had unwittingly birthed a monster in DeeDee, one that would not simply fade away.

Delores decides to reach out to someone she hasn't spoken to in over twenty years but she's desperate, "Hello Pam, it's Delores."

"Well, after all these years, you decide to call me."

"I heard Terri and the baby were in a car accident, and I thought you might have heard more."

"If I had heard more, I wouldn't have called to tell you."

"Why not? I'm her mother, and that is my grandson."

"Delores cut the bullshit and save the theatrics; you know damn well you don't care about those children; you and your daughter are looking for a way to get in and get her money."

Delores takes a breath. She does not want conflict. "Pam, why can't we have a civil conversation for the sake of Terri?"

Pam chuckles, "I would love to have a civil conversation with you, but I'm afraid we've passed that; therefore, I have nothing to say to you."

Delores ignores the sarcasm, "Are you on your way to Boston?"

"Indeed, I am. That's my niece. She's like a daughter to me and besides, someone from her family needs to be by her side."

Delores wants to curse Pam out, but she knows that would be senseless.

"Pam despite what you think and what you think you know, I love Terri."

"Delores, I have no intention of listening to you lie and try to convince yourself of the lie. This is getting old, real old, so please stop. My plane is almost gassed up. I would ask if you needed a ride, but I don't feel like being inconvenienced; this call was my limit for today."

Pam hangs up on Delores and makes another call, "Is he ready?"

"Yes, I have him dressed and ready," says Anne.

Meanwhile, Delores decides to go to Boston and check on Terri, but she needs DeeDee's help.

"DeeDee," yells Delores as she enters the main house.

"Mama, why are you yelling throughout my house."

"Terri and the baby have been in a bad car accident, and I need to get to her as soon as possible."

DeeDee yarns, "Excuse me, so what do you want me to do?"

"I want you to book me a flight to Boston so I can go up there and check on her, and I want you to come with me."

DeeDee shakes her head no, "I'm not going up there; what about my job."

"Your job, that is your sister!"

"Who has a baby with my husband? I'm not forgetting that." DeeDee walks into the kitchen and starts her coffee.

"If you want to be mad, be mad with me, it was all me; I sat you and Quincey up to be together."

"I am mad with you, Quincey, and Terri, I feel like it's me against the world right now."

For The Sake of Love II

"Can we deal with your feelings after we get back from Boston?'

As she sips her coffee, DeeDee thinks, "Okay, I'll go because if she dies, I want to make sure she leaves me her money." DeeDee walks into her office and makes trip reservations for her and Delores.

Delores returns to her mother-in-law's house and packs for the trip. She hears her cell phone ring, but when she looks at the caller ID, it's a blocked number; she reluctantly answers, "Hello."

"I'll do whatever it takes to protect my husband's reputation; you're next."

The person hangs up.

Delores is terrified. "Oh my God, that was Mrs. Phillips. " She tries to track the call, but she can't retrieve the phone number.

Back at the hospital,

Terri is sitting in the ICU with her son when Kamal walks in; Terri jumps up and grabs onto him, "Our baby." Terri is crying.

Kamal holds on to her, "shhhhhh, he's going to be okay."

Kamal looks at his son, his head bandaged, and his body is still.

"Look at me, we must pray for our baby, and pray he will get through this, and I promise you no matter what we are going to get through this."

For The Sake of Love II

"I'm not going to get through this if my only son dies," in an instant, Terri thinks about Martin.

"We are going to think positive," The two of them sit down next to their son.

Nina is still in the lobby, she's nervous and needs someone to talk to so she calls Otichia and Devonna so they can calm her.

Otichia and Martin moved together into Martin's apartment; Otichia is renting her house for extra income, "Martin, I have to go to the hospital, Terri was in a car accident," says Otichia.

"What, what do you mean, is she okay," Martin is noticeably freaking out.

"Calm down honey, I know she's your boss, but you seem to have a personal thing for her I noticed."

"No, I'm going with you," martin grabs his keys, I'll drive."

The two leave out of the house to get into Martin's car when shots ring out, "pow, pow, pow,"

Otichia is hit by gunfire in her side, and Martin is hit on the arm, "Help me, help me," screams Otichia.

Martin grabs his cell phone, to call 911, and he sees a truck speeding off. "Hello, I need the police," he gives the address, "My girlfriend and I have been shot."

Otichia is losing a lot of blood, "Martin, don't let me die."

"Baby, I got you," Martin looks down at her side and shakes his head. Where is the ambulance?" he says under his breath.

"Finally, he can hear the loud sirens from the ambulance coming down their street, "Baby, you hear them; they are on the way."

Otichia can hear them, but her pulse is starting to faint because she is losing blood.

The medics jump out of the ambulance, rush over to Otichia, and start working on her.

Martin wants to leave and check on Terri.

"Let me check your arm," says the medic.

"I'm okay, the bullet t grazed me, I'll be okay, Just," he breaks down but fights back his tears. "Please help her."

The police arrive and want to question Martin.

"Excuse me, sir, we need to ask you some questions, "Do you know who would want to kill you or your wife?"

"No, and she's not my wife; she's my girlfriend, and we don't have any enemies."

"Where were you on your way to," asks the officer.

"She got a phone call from a friend that their friend was in a bad car accident, and we were on our way to the hospital, and when we approached the car that's when some idiot started shooting."

"Did you see anything?"

"Yes, I saw a navy blue pickup truck speeding away."

"Did you see who was driving it?"

"No, but I did see the passenger, he was a Black male, bald head with a black jacket on."

"Thank you, sir, we are going to question the neighbors while you and your girlfriend go to the hospital."

Back in Ohio

DeeDee has made flight reservations, and she is packing and thinking about the weather in Boston this time of year. She wants to make sure she takes the right clothes. The thought of Terri in an accident hasn't crossed her mind.

There's a knock on the door, DeeDee stops and answers the door."

It's two white police officers, "Hello Ma'am.

DeeDee is nervous. She starts thinking about the money she took from Terri and stutters, "H h h, how can I help you?"

"Ma'am are you Ms. Hightower,

"Why says DeeDee standing in a pair of black leggings and a black t-shirt that says "Black lives matter" in glitter.

"Ma'am there's been an accident,"

"We know about the accident, but why are you here? The accident happened in Boston."

Another officer stepped up "Hello, ma'am. I am Officer Parham. May I speak to Mrs. Hightower?"

DeeDee's tone changes, "this is her; what can I do for you?"

"Ma'am, may we come in?"

"No, you may not, do you have a warrant or something." DeeDee's is fidgety

"No ma'am, we have some news about your husband."

"My ex-husband, you mean."

"He has you listed as the next of kin."

"Wait a minute," DeeDee thinks to herself. This sounds serious." She lets them in, "Okay, come on in, and I have a gun, and it is licensed."

"Thanks for letting us know, "Ma'am, I don't know how to say this, but just to say it, your husband is dead, I mean your ex-husband."

DeeDee wasn't expecting that. She grabbed her chest, her heart beating fast, and a sunken feeling hit her stomach." Wait what?" "I need to sit down, mama!" she yelled for Delores.

DeeDee is surprisingly upset, "What happened," she starts crying, "Mama, come here now!"

The police help DeeDee sit on the couch; Ma'am, we know it's a lot.

For The Sake of Love II

Delores walks into the living room just as the police are helping DeeDee sit down. "Get your hands off of my daughter!"

"Mama, it's okay; Chauncey is dead; they came to tell me Chauncey is dead."

"Dead, what happened," Delores sits next to DeeDee and places her arms around her.

"His car blew up and after the firefighters investigated, his car was bombed."

"Bombed, oh no," Delores jumps up, "are you saying someone tried to kill him?"

"Yes, ma'am that is exactly what we're saying, and that is why we're here also. We want to ask questions."

DeeDee looks up at the police officer, "What type of questions, you don't think I did it, do you?"

"Ma'am, we are not accusing you; we're just here to ask questions. We spoke with his family and friends, and they told us that your divorce was messy."

"Get out of my house, you came here to see if I killed him. I am not a murderer, and he is the father of my children; we have two beautiful kids together."

"Ma'am, we just want to ask a few questions."

"Let them ask the questions, DeeDee," says Delores.

DeeDee squeezes her lips and rolls her eyes, "Okay, ask."

"Where were you yesterday around 11 am?"

DeeDee thinks, I was getting an oil change and then I stopped at the grocery store."

"When was the last time you saw Mr. Hightower?"

"He stopped by last week to talk about…" she stops talking.

The police officer looks up from his notepad, "is there something else."

DeeDee stutters, "n n n no there's nothing else."

Delores's eyeball is jumping out of the socket, "Don't say anything else."

DeeDee yanks away from her mother, "I didn't kill him, and I have nothing to hide."

DeeDee looks at the police, "We argued because he wanted to sell this house, my house, our house and he wanted me to move, and I didn't want to move."

Delores puts her forehead on her hand, "Oh Jesus, please shut her up."

"Ma'am we have a few more questions, and then we're done."

Delores takes over, "No this is over now, if you have more questions, she needs her lawyer present." She looks at DeeDee, "You're done."

The police officer looks around the room.

"What are you looking for, a bomb," asks DeeDee.

Delores almost has a heart attack, "will you shut the hell up."

The police leave.

Delores peeps out of the curtain and waits until she sees the police pull off before she starts talking to DeeDee.

"Mama, why are you acting like that?"

"Girl, you are the dumbest child. You have the looks, but you are slow as a crockpot. Terri would have told them where to go and how to get there."

"What are you talking about? What did I do wrong?"

"You are a suspect, dummy."

"No, I'm not, and besides, I still love Chauncey. Why would I kill him."

"That's exactly why, because you still love him!" Delores is frustrated, she begins pacing the floor.

"You are confusing me, and I have no time for this, I have to contact my children and Chauncey's family. I can't go and check on Terri with you."

Delores shakes her head, "That's what I get for having a baby by a man that would rob a bank," she says under her breath.

DeeDee walks back into her room and starts to unpack while calling her children.

Delores follows her into her bedroom, "Hang up, we need to talk."

"Mama, I don't have time, I am calling the kids. I don't want the police telling my children their father is dead."

Delores grabs DeeDee's phone, "Listen to me, I think I know who killed him."

"Who, and why didn't you tell the police."

"I can't because I'm not one hundred percent sure, but I think Mrs. Phillips had him killed and had Terri hurt, too."

DeeDee gives her mother a crazy look, "Mama, you're being melodramatic."

"Shut up and listen, and stop using words you can't even spell."

DeeDee doesn't realize she's just been insulted.

"When I went into my house, I got a call from Mrs. Phillips and she said, "I will protect my husband's reputation. It went something like that."

"So, what does that mean?"

"God help me with her!"

"It means that she is going to silence anyone who can tell he husband the truth about Martin and who his parents are."

"What, that is silly," DeeDee laughs.

"Who would want Chauncey dead, can you answer that? Chauncey was a nice man; he stayed to himself, and his family owned a church. Chauncey is a good guy."

"If he were that good guy, he would have stayed with his wife and children."

"You're not the nicest person to love."

Now DeeDee is insulted, "and who's fault is that? Because you raised me, it's not like I had a dad like Terri to leave me millions."

"Okay, let's calm down. I am sure Mrs. Phillips is behind this, and that could only mean one thing."

"What's that," asks DeeDee.

"I'm next on the list."

Back in Boston at the hospital.

Martin and Otichia are taken to the same emergency room where Terri, Kamal and the baby are at.

Otichia is in critical condition, but Martin has a superficial wound, and he is okay. The doctors sew him up with a few stitches. Martin starts looking for answers, but first, he wants to check on Terri.

He walks up to the nurse's station and asks for Terri Dozier, "Excuse me can you page Terri Dozier."

The nurse pages Terri to the front.

"Who could be paging me," asks Terri.

"I'll go and see you sit right here," says Kamal.

Kamal walks out to the nurse's station and sees Martin; he looks at his arm and says, " Hey, are you okay?"

"No, man, shit is bad, somebody shot at me and Otichia, and she was hit in the side. The doctors are working on her now. I need to call her family, but I wanted to check on Terri."

Kamal can't believe what he's hearing, "what in the hell is going on? A car hit Terri and the baby and sped off."

"So, it was deliberate," asked Martin.

"I don't know, I just don't know," says Kamal.

Terri walks out of the room and to the nurse's station after Kamal doesn't return; she sees Martin, "What's going on? What happened to you."

Martin can't say anything, so he stares at her.

"Talk to me," says Terri."

"Otichia was shot; someone shot at us."

"What, where is she? Are you okay," she looks at Kamal, Baby, what is happening?"

"She's in there now; the doctors are trying to get the bullet out."

Meanwhile, Nina is in the waiting area with Devonna, and they don't know what happened with Otichia.

Back in Ohio.

Auntie Pam and the other passengers board her private plane.

"Are you okay," asks Pam.

"I'm fine, but where are we going to?"

"We're going to visit family; it's time."

"Okay, whatever you say."

DeeDee and Delores

DeeDee phones her children, who are away at college, and delivers the devastating news that their father has passed away, urging them to return home as soon as possible.

Delores is extremely upset that DeeDee didn't wait for the children to arrive before breaking the news to them, and she is convinced that Ms. Phillips has arranged for someone to harm Chauncey and Terri, and she may be next.

By this time, Nina and Devonna had heard about what had happened to Otichia and Martin.

Delores calls Nina.

"Hello, Ms. Delores,"

"Hello, have you heard any updates on Terri and the baby?"

Terri and Kamal are still in ICU with the baby; she came out to tell us that the baby is stable; they had to put him in a coma for now."

"Okay, thank you. I have a flight, and I should be there in the morning."

"Terri will need all the family support she can get. Will DeeDee be coming with you?"

Delores thought it odd of her to ask about DeeDee. No, she's not coming; she just received some bad news about her husband."

"I guess it's a lot going around; we just got bad news about our friend Otichia and her boyfriend, Martin."

"Oh no, I'm sorry to hear that," Delores doesn't realize what Martin Nina is talking about."

"It's really sad to hear someone would just start shooting at them."

"Shooting, someone shot at Otichia and her boyfriend."

"Yes, right in front of Martin's home."

Now it's starting to click: "Is Martin the same guy who works at Terri's marketing firm?"

"Yes, he and Otichia have been dating for a while now, and…."

Delores hung up on her, "It's true, she is trying to kill us." Delores is panicking.

Nina looks at her phone after a period of silence, "the call dropped."

"She wants us dead, all of us, that means I'm next." Delores rushes into the main house to talk to DeeDee, but DeeDee is not there.

Delores looks out of the window and DeeDee's car is gone, "Oh no, I'm here by myself and DeeDee is out there." Delores thinks, "Have to get in touch with Mrs.

Phillips; "if she wants a war, I'm going to give her a motherfucking war."

Delores looks for Ms. Phillips's phone number and calls her.

"You are getting my message, I see," says Ms. Phillips.

"I put it together, and your phone call this morning helped me put the pieces together. I'm warning you: stop this madness, or you are going to cause a lot of bodies to drop."

"I told you if he ever found out that I would make you pay."

"Make me pay and leave my family alone; this is between me and you."

"Not anymore," Mrs. Phillips coughs,"

"Look at you, you're sick and dying and you're trying to take my family with you."

"I will not go to my grave with my husband, knowing Martin is not his father; you will not tarnish my reputation and hurt my husband."

"I'm warning you, leave my family alone…"

"Or what, Delores, what can you do? You're broke and broken; you sold your grandson to me for murder and money, and now you're worried about family. You are just what the Dozier's said you are, trash."

"I'm going to show you how trash cleans up." Delores hangs up the phone.

Ms. Phillips's phone rings, "What do you want."

"he's still alive, ma'am."

"Well, finish the goddamn job." Ms. Phillips hangs up the phone.

Delores calls DeeDee. She pats her feet while she sits at the kitchen table, "Answer the phone, DeeDee."

"Hello,"

"Where are you,"

"I left to go to the store and get food for the kids and Chauncey's family; they are coming over."

"No, they can't come here," says Delores.

"Mama, stop being silly. I called them, and his parents and family are coming to the house so we can talk and make plans."

"DeeDee, listen to me; someone is trying to kill us, all of us."

DeeDee had hung up.

For The Sake of Love II

Back in Boston.

Otichia's family arrived at the hospital, and after the bullet was taken out, the doctors said she would be fine. In the meantime, the police are questioning Martin.

Pam's plane touches down on the tarmac, and a gust of Boston wind tousles her elegant silver bob. She deftly secures her sunglasses on top of her head, keeping her hair away from her face. A waiting car promptly whisks her away to the hospital, where she is eager to visit Terri and the newborn baby.

Pam is concerned about how their arrival may affect Terri, but deep down, she feels like she's doing the right thing at the right time.

Kamal's mother and sister, Carla, are at the hospital in the waiting area.

The doctor walks into the room and talks to Kamal and Terri,

Both are nervous, "yes, doctor, is he going to be okay," asks Kamal.

"You have a strong baby, and he is a fighter, but right now, it will be touch and go."

Terri breaks down crying, "he's just a baby."

"Babies bounce back better than adults. We are keeping a close eye on him and are going to do everything to get him through this."

After exiting the room, Terri and Kamal join their families, friends, and Otichia's family in the waiting area.

They all can't believe this is happening.

Back in Ohio.

An hour has slipped by, and a gnawing worry settles in Delores's stomach as she glances at her phone. She's tried calling DeeDee several times now, but each attempt has ended with the ringing cut off and a frustrating leap straight to voicemail.

Hoping to find some answers, Delores decides to reach out to others. Mr. Phillips is at the top of her list, but when she calls, Mrs. Phillips picks up, leaving Delores with silence on the other end as there's no response to her eagerness.

For The Sake of Love II

Back in Boston.

Pam's car pulls up at the hospital, and they are ushered into a private entrance reserved for the rich and famous.

"We're almost there, just a few more steps," says Pam.

Pam called ahead and asked the nurse to take Terri to a private room to wait for her.

Terri wanted Kamal and all the other family members and friends to come with her and wait for Pam to arrive.

Terri has her back to the elevator door when it opens, and her Aunt Pam steps off, "Terri,"

Terri turns around, "he gasps,"

"I have someone I want you to see,"

"Oh my God, oh my God," says Terri.

Kamal looks, "What, what is wrong?"

"It can't be," Terri walks closer, "Daddy."

"Yes, it's your father."

The big, tall, strong man Terri remembers is now seventy-eight years old, shorter than she is, and looks weak, "How can this be Auntie Pam?" She doesn't take her eyes off her dad.

"We'll talk about that later," Pam winks at Terri.

"Hi baby girl," Gary's voice is low.

Terri leans over his wheelchair and hugs him. Tears flow from her eyes. "Daddy, I have missed you, I have needed you." Terri kisses his cheeks.

Martin steps up from behind everyone, he looks, he hesitates at first and then, "Is he my grandfather,"

Everyone gasps and whispers, "What."

Terri looks at Martin, "Yes, yes, this is my daddy and your grandfather."

Martin walks closer to Terri, and for the second time in his life, Terri hugs him. "I am your mother, and I have waited thirty-seven years to say that."

Everyone standing around is in shock and they don't have a clue as to what is going on.

Chapter Two

Choose who you love

For The Sake of Love II

Back in Ohio

Delores called Mr. Phillips three times, but she hasn't been able to reach him. His secretary says he's not in.

DeeDee left to go to the grocery store over four hours ago, and Delores is worried something may have happened to her. She called her cell phone, and it's now going straight to voice mail.

Delores peeps out of the kitchen window, she feels like a sitting duck waiting to be shot at, "Please don't let anything happen to my baby," Delores is so nervous her hands are shaking.

A few hours later.

Delores's cell phone rings, "Hello," she answers without looking at the number.

"Hi grandma, we're here but our mother isn't here to pick us up."

"Okay, take a lip and I'll pay for it."

Her granddaughter laughs, "Grandma, it's a Lyft."

Delores is in no mood to be corrected. "Okay, whatever. You and your brother get here, and don't make any stops anywhere else."

"Grandma is something going on because you sound weird."

Delores pauses, takes a deep breath, and says, with a lowered voice, "I'll be waiting for you, honey."

Delores walks back to the window and gently lifts the mini blind to look out. This time, she sees a black four-door car with tinted windows. Her heart jumps, "That car wasn't there before."

Delores tries to call DeeDee again, "Answer the phone DeeDee,"

The call goes to voice mail again, and Delores starts crying, "Something is wrong; I can feel it."

Mrs. Phillips has Delores by the neck, and she is choking the life out of her and her family.

Delores hears a car pull up, she jumps up and runs over to the window; it's her grandchildren.

The car with the tinted windows is still sitting in front of their house.

Delores quickly opens the door, "come on, hurry up," she yells.

The children run into the house with their bags, asking, "Grandma, what is going on, and where is Mom?"

"I don't know where your mom is," her voice cracks, I think something happened to her."

"Something like what, grandma, what is going on, for real? Our father is dead and now mom isn't answering her phone."

Delores's cell phone rings, "wait let me get this"

"Hello,"

"Mother my phone died, are the children there yet."

"Oh Jesus, thank God you're alive; yes, the kids are here."

DeeDee doesn't say anything else."

"We've been trying to call you, but your phone went to voice mail. What is taking you so long?"

"I'm buying food down the street from Walmart, Mother."

Delores thought it odd that DeeDee called her mother "Mother; she never calls me that."

"Are you sure you're okay because you sound weird and where is down the street?"

"Mother, I'm fine and I'll be home shortly."

DeeDee hangs up the phone, but Delores holds her cell phone up to her ear. " Something's wrong; I can feel it," Delores says to herself.

Delores is suspicious, "DeeDee never calls me mother. Something is definitely going on, and it's not good."

"Where are you taking me," says DeeDee"

A tall black man with bulging muscles out of his black T-shirt grabs DeeDee's arm and says, " Shut up and get in the car."

"Wait, I have nothing to do with what's going on."

"Oh well," the man is not concerned.

DeeDee is scared out of her mind; she doesn't know what will happen to her.

Back at the house, Delores can't calm down. She's pacing the floor, but she doesn't want her grandchildren to sense it.

Time is ticking away, and with every hour that passes, Delores fears the worst. She tries to reach out to Mr. Phillips again, but that doesn't work. She needs to come up with a plan.

Delores's granddaughter walks into the room where Delores is sitting, "Grandma, where is our mother and what is going on; I'm getting a weird feeling."

Delores doesn't know what to say; her stomach is in knots. "Everything is going to be okay. Maybe she's buying some extra stuff. You know how your mother is."

Delores needs something to keep her from losing her mind, so she starts cooking dinner. After a few hours, she cooks a Thanksgiving meal, and finally, her phone rings.

"Hello, Mrs. Phillips."

"Yes, Delores, I have your daughter and will release her for you, my driver will come and pick you up and drop your daughter off."

"Stop anything you want; just don't hurt my daughter."

"You are the only person that can prove that Martin is not my husband's child."

"That's not true; Terri and Martin can take a DNA test."

"I've taken care of them."

Delores gets a lump in her throat; she hasn't talked to Terri since the accident, so she doesn't know what is going on with her. "You killed Terri?" Delores starts crying.

"I'm tying up loose ends as we speak."

"Okay, I'll do it, just tell me where and when and I'll do it," says Delores.

"Delores, you know I am not a fool, so if you call the police or make any moves, just remember I have eyes on you. Do you see the car outside with the tinted windows?"

Delores walks back into the living room and looks out of the window, "yes," her voice trembles.

"They are trained killers, so don't try anything, or everyone in the house dies."

"No problem, come and get me; just don't hurt my daughter."

Mrs. Phillips gets mad, "I'm calling the shots here, not you!"

"Okay, I'm sorry; I just don't want anyone else to get hurt; you are hurting innocent people."

"No, I'm hurting people that could make me lose everything!"

Delores realizes she's not getting through to Mrs. Phillips.

"Once I see that my daughter is safe, then and only then will I agree to leave with your hitmen, and I promise I won't make any moves or call anyone. you have my word."

"If it were all about your word, we wouldn't be in this mess."

"My grandson went looking for his birth parents, I had nothing to do with that."

"He is not your grandson; he is my son!"

"I'm sorry, you're right."

"You were a struggling nobody when I met you, and I took you in like a sister and a friend. I took you in and took your children on expensive vacations. I treated you like family, and this is how you repay me; you betrayed me."

"But, I haven't done anything; I kept my mouth closed; this is not on me."

Mrs. Phillips hangs up the phone and looks at Delores, "It's a shame how easy you were willing to give up your mother," she laughs, "but she is willing to lay down her life for you."

Twenty-four hours later

DeeDee is back home with her children, and Delores is locked up in Mrs. Phillips's basement scared to death.

Mrs. Phillips sits on her beautifully decorated deck, enveloped in a luxurious Chanel throw blanket, gazing out at the ever-changing sky; she finds herself humming a soothing tune. Despite her present circumstances, observing the shifting clouds brings her a profound sense of peace.

"Hello,"

Mrs. Phillips turns her wheelchair around and is startled. "Oh goodness, Martin, you scared me. How long have you been standing there?"

"Not long, "Mr. Phillips doesn't move as fast as he used to, but for a seventy-five-year-old man, he gets around fairly well.

He walks over to his wife and leans over her, "What are you up to now."

"What are you talking about? I'm not up to anything."

Mr. Phillips gazes deeply into his wife's eyes, studying the gentle creases on her face, the soft strands of white hair, and the subtle tremor of her head. "I know better than anyone."

"You don't know anything, and how could you? You're never here; you're gone all the time to DC and Virginia, and I know it's not just for work. It's work and play and a lot of play; she looks at him and sees the same man she married, tall, strong, and handsome. Her love for him has no end, and she would do anything to keep him.

"You know I have provided you with everything you ever wanted. You have lived better than you would have had I left you in Maryland with your family in a two-bedroom apartment."

Mrs. Phillips sits quietly, listening as he talks; however, her mind is wandering.

"Do you think I don't know what goes on in my house, the house I built for you," his voice gets loud.

"Mrs. Phillips is nervous, "what are you babbling about, Martin."

"I don't babble, and do you know why?" he walks up close to his wife, "because I am a United States senator!"

"Okay, honey, I know that." Mrs. Phillips is scared.

"No, you don't because if you did you wouldn't have people run off the road, kidnapped, blowing up cars, or having our son shot at!"

Mrs. Phillips gasps, "M m m m m m, Martin, wait, I don't know what you're talking about."

"You know exactly what I'm talking about. Don't sit there playing innocently with me. I know everything that goes on in this house, I always have, and I always will!"

"I'm cold. Can you turn on the fireplace? " Mrs. Phillips asks, wanting to change the subject.

"No, it's not cold in here," he says, walking over to her and pointing at her heart. "It's cold in there."

Mrs. Phillips starts to cry, "What is wrong with you? You're abusing me; I am a defenseless old woman; how dare you treat me like this."

"Cut the bullshit, I know the stuff you have been doing, and it stops right now, and do you know why? I'll tell you why. Because the people you hired to do your dirty work report to me. Delores has been returned to her family."

Mrs. Phillips gasps, "What are you talking about?

Cut the Bull; It's time we got this over and done with," he says, unloosening his tie, taking off his suit jacket and lighting a cigar.

"Do you know why we don't have any other children besides Martin Jr?"

"Yes, because I had problems conceiving."

Mr. Phillips laughs, "Is that what you think?"

"Yes, that's the truth. After Martin was born, I couldn't get pregnant again." Mrs. Phillips's eyes dance back and forth; she doesn't understand where this conversation is going.

"No, that's not it," Mr. Phillips sits down on the lounge chair so he can be at eye level with his wife, and he leans forward. No, no, no that's not our case."

"What on earth are you talking about? You are scaring me; I don't like this, Martin."

"After your last miscarriage before Martin, I went to the doctors and got a vasectomy."

She cuts him off, "You're lying; why would you do that."

"I didn't want to have any more children."

Mrs. Phillips cuts him off again. "Martin, you sound ridiculous. Stop it!" She's getting agitated. "I need my medicine."

"No, what you need is to hear the truth."

Mrs. Phillips tries to roll her wheelchair past her husband, but he stops her, "You're going to sit here and listen to me."

"Martin, stop talking crazy. You're old and feeble, and you don't know what you're talking about."

"Okay, I guess I just have to say it," Mr. Phillips stands up, "I know Martin Jr. is not my son."

Mrs. Phillips gasps, "You have lost your mind, talking that foolishness to me. Martin Jr is the spitting image of you."

"No, he's the spitting image of someone else, but not me and you know that."

Mrs. Phillips starts coughing and coughing. She reaches out for her husband's hand, but he pulls away from her. "Help me, I need some water."

Mr. Phillips opens a water bottle for her and hands it to her. "Here you go because there's more, lots more."

Mrs. Phillips drinks the water, her hands shaking from the anxiety and shock, she sips the water, and her coughing stops.

"Okay, can I proceed because I need you to be clear about this conversation?"

She doesn't say anything.

"Okay, the year before Martin was born, I had a daughter with one of my interns and right after that, I had twins, a son, and a daughter with Kelly."

"Kelly, our housekeeper!"

"Yes,"

"You got that white girl pregnant?"

"Yes,"

"You son-of-a-bitch,"

"Who are you to judge; you sit in that chair still lying to me about a son that isn't mine."

"That's a lie; he is our son. Do you hear me? He is our son!" Mrs. Phillips starts coughing again.

A smug look on his face, his hands behind his back, "At first, I said, "Maybe she had an affair," but I know you, you wouldn't. So, I started doing some investigating, and I have to say you were very sloppy and left a trail of evidence. First, you took a lump sum of money out of the bank right after Martin was born. Secondly, Delores quit working for me abruptly, and she started spending money around town, and the streets were talking about her pregnant teenage daughter; and last but not least, you paid for a murder for hire on one of the richest men in the United States."

"Martin, you are talking ridiculous; I did no such thing."

"To make a long story short, I knew Martin Jr was not my son all these years, and I said nothing because I knew you were desperately trying to have a child and couldn't. I felt guilty that I had children with other women, so I said nothing."

"You bastard you," she coughs, "You cheated on me?"

"Did you really think I was going to live without children, an heir to my legacy?"

"You mother fucker, I loved you, and I would have done anything to keep us together, and that baby was to keep us together."

"No, dear, that baby was to keep you away from me while I lived my life the way I wanted to. I played the game with you, but I knew that boy wasn't my son from day one."

Mrs. Phillips tries to stand up, and she lunges at Mr. Phillips.

He steps back just in time.

Her body hits the floor, "Help me, Martin, help me," she cries out, and begs him.

"Your choices are to go to prison and live out your last days or leave Delores and her family alone and let them be."

"They are trying to ruin our family, Martin, I can't let them do that. Please help me up,"

Mr. Phillips leans down over her body, "I lived with your lie for three decades; let Martin Jr have his family and leave those people alone.

"You and Delores can go to hell," says Mrs. Phillips.

Mr. Phillips turns to leave.

"Martin, Martin, please don't leave me here to die; I love you; I love you."

Mr. Phillips walks back to her and helps her into the wheelchair.

As he helps her, she smacks him across the face, "Do you think I'm a fool? I knew about the son and the twins. You fool, I got phone calls from both of them bragging about how they slept with my husband, but I wasn't going anywhere. I told them you got babies, but I will always be his wife."

"You purchased a baby to keep me."

"No fool, I purchased a baby to keep me living well."

"You bought a baby to save yourself because you were afraid that I would take all of this away from you?"

She chuckles and then coughs, "When I met you in Maryland, you were a Geechee from Alabama, going to school to be a lawyer. I made you the man the women loved because when you walked into the courtroom, it was my swag; when you became a Senator, it was my confidence. Without me, you would have been a nobody. I made you, and I wasn't going to let your indiscretions bother me. Your affairs and children are no bother to me."

"I am my own man," he yells at her.

"I let you think that."

Mr. Phillips starts choking his wife."

She tried to pry his hands from around her neck, but she was too weak, "Help, help me," no one heard her.

The next morning.

Delores woke from the nightmare and looked around; she was in her bed. She through the covers off and ran to the main house looking for DeeDee and the children.

DeeDee was up cooking breakfast, and as Delores approached the house, she smelled the eggs, French toast and bacon.

DeeDee singing.

"DeeDee," Delores tapped her on her shoulder."

DeeDee was startled, "Mom, what are you doing here."

"What do you mean, I live here."

"No, No, I mean I thought Mrs. Phillips," she stopped.

"Mr. Phillips came and he released me. I was scared for my life. Did you call the police."

DeeDee looked dumb founded, "Well no, I was told not to or they would harm me and the children."

For The Sake of Love II

"So your dumb ass was going to let her kill me?" Delores was furious with DeeDee. "I created a monster."

"What do you mean," asked DeeDee.

Delores left and walked back to her house.

DeeDee walked behind her, trying to get answers, "What is wrong? You're home and alive."

"Yes, but no thanks to you." Delores started packing.

"Where are you going."

I'm going to be with your sister and my two grandsons."

"But I need you here with me. I have a funeral to plan, and I need you."

"DeeDee," Delores starts crying, " Terri needs me. I have done this too long, and it's time I stopped. I need, no I want to be a mother to both of my daughters."

DeeDee has an attitude, "You can catch a cab to the airport," DeeDee walks away.

Delores watches as she walks away and shakes her head, "DeeDee, DeeDee," she calls out.

DeeDee ignores her and walks away.

Delores makes a call, "Hello, thank you for saving me, I didn't know what she was going to do to me."

"No problem, you won't have any more problems from here on out."

For The Sake of Love II

Delores calls a cab to leave.

The cab pulls up, "I'm leaving,"
The grandchildren walk her to the cab while DeeDee peeps through the blinds watching.

Delores looks back, but she can't see DeeDee watching.

Chapter Three

Secrets from the Grave

For The Sake of Love II

4 days after Terri's accident.

Delores's plane lands in Boston. She calls Terri again, but there is no answer, so she decides to call Nina.

Nina answers, excited by all that is taking place at the hospital, "Hello"

Delores is startled; she can hear the commotion in the background, "Nina, is everything alright? I've been trying to reach Terri?"

Nina holds her phone close to her ear and places her finger in her other ear to drown out the loud talking in the background, "We're all at the hospital still, and the baby is doing okay. The doctors are hopeful."

"My flight just landed, and I don't want to catch a taxi to someplace. I don't know where I'm going, so can someone pick me up?"

"I'll have a car sent to you to pick you up," says Nina.

Delores is insulted, "A car? Where are my daughter and her fiancé?"

Nina picks up on her attitude, "They both want to stay at the hospital with their son just in case the doctors need them, Ms. Delores." Nina shoots the tone right back at her.

"Okay, fine, I'm at gate D3."

"I'll send a car to pick you up."

"Wait a minute, how will they know me, and how will I know them? I don't get into random cars."

Nina breathes, "You're right. What are you wearing? I need to let the driver know."

Delores describes what she is wearing to Nina.

"I'll let the driver know and they should be there shortly."

Nina hangs up the phone. "Should I tell Terri her mother is on the way, or not. She stands to the side, watching Terri, Terri's dad, and Terri's auntie talk in a huddle. "No, I'll just wait until she gets here."

In the meantime

Martin and Otichia's family are talking to the police about the shooting and why it occurred. The police have no suspects; however, they do have video footage they are reviewing. Otichia's family suspects Martin may be into drugs and other stuff, and that's why they were shot at.

Martin tries to explain to her family that he doesn't know what is going on, but he assures them that he has nothing to do with it and he is not a drug dealer. Martin is just as anxious as they are to get to the bottom of what happened.

A Police Officer was assigned to Otichia's room in case someone tried to finish attacking her again.

Terri is still in shock after seeing her father; so many years have passed without him in her life. She knew she would never see him again, at least not on this side. Terri has a lot of questions and doesn't know where to start.

For The Sake of Love II

Delores is still at the airport, waiting for her ride and thinking about the last few days. "A lot has happened in the last few days, but thank God it's over. I don't have to worry about Mrs. Phillips, and DeeDee is okay," she looks at her watch, "I need to get to Terri and make things right with her."

A car pulls up, "Excuse me, are you Ms. Delores?"

"Yes,"

The driver gets out, grabs her bags, and opens the door for her.

Delores feels uneasy and suddenly becomes nervous. "Why am I feeling like this? I hope everything is okay with the baby."

After a short ride, the driver pulls up at the hospital. The driver opens the door and hands her the suitcase, saying, "Have a great day, ma'am."

"I'm getting out in front of a hospital, and you're telling me to have a great day; what an idiot." Delores doesn't know where to go. She calls Terri, and again, there is no answer. "What is she doing?"

Nina calls Delores's phone, "Where are you."

"I'm here, but I don't know where to go. Can you come and get me?"

"Sure, I'll be right down, says Nina." Ninna whispers to Devonna that she's leaving to pick up Terri's mother.

"Okay," says Devonna.

Nina catches the elevator to the lobby. As soon as she steps off the elevator, she sees Ms. Delores. "Ms. Delores, hi,"

"Hello, how is Terri and the baby?

"The baby is doing a lot better after surgery; however, the doctors say he may not be the same after the accident."

Delores grabs her chest and stops walking, "what are you saying."

"Little Gary may have special needs."

"Oh my God, Terri's only child and now this, and I don't know why she gave him that old name, Gary. That's a name for an old ass man."

"She loves her father, and she wanted to honor him," says Nina.

"She could have honored him another way; besides, he's dead."

"That's what we all thought," says Nina.

"Girl, what on earth are you talking about? The man is dead."

The elevator doors open, and Terri, Kamal, Kamal's family, Devonna, Auntie Pam, and the nurses look toward the elevator.

Delores's eyes popped open; she could see everyone staring at her, and it felt weird.

For The Sake of Love II

Delores walks off the elevator and runs to Terri and Kamal, "How is the baby? I got here as soon as I could."

Terri doesn't say anything right away; she looks at her mother.

Auntie Pam looks Delores up and down, "It took you four days to get here?"

"I'm here for my daughter and grandson; I'm in no mood for foolishness, Pam."

"You could have fooled me."

"Mama so much has happened," Terri tears up, "The baby, my adult son, and my father."

"What, what are you talking about? Are you okay," asks Delores.

"Hello, grandma," says Martin.

A cold feeling came over Delores, and goose bumps lined up and down her arms, "I'm not your grandmother, boy."

"I'm not a boy; I'm a man, and you are indeed my grandmother. I'm the son you sold to the Phillips."

Delores looks around the room at everyone who is looking at her. Her breathing becomes heavy, and her nostrils flare.

"Is that Delores's voice I hear," says Gary as his nurse rolls him back into the waiting room from the bathroom.

Delores turns and sees the man who was the love of her life sitting in a wheelchair and alive. Delores faints,"

"Someone get a doctor," yells Devonna.

"For what? Let that bitch die," says Auntie Pam.

"Auntie Pam, nooooo, she's still my mother," says Terri.

"The same mother that sold your son and had a hitman shoot my brother."

"What, Auntie Pam, what are you talking about," asked Terri.

Everyone was quiet, and Devonna and Nina couldn't believe what they heard.

"Rich people got more problems than we do," says Devonna.

"You don't know half of it; somebody has been stealing money from Terri's account and using her credit cards," says Nina.

"Girl, you are lying," says Devonna.

"I wish I were, and it's somebody in this room."

"Wait a minute, we got a murderer and a thief in this room?"

"Yep," says Nina.

"I'm getting my ass outta here before I get killed," Devonna was serious.

"No, don't leave me here; you and I are the only ones that ain't got shit to do with this stuff."

"Exactly, and we'll be the ones dying in here," says Devonna.

"Shhhhhhhh, be quiet, listen and watch because I got the feeling some more bombs will be dropped today," says Nina.

Devonna and Nina sit in the front row and watch as the nurses try to help Delores regain her strength.

Two nurses assist Delores; one nurse takes her vitals while another gives her a glass of water.

Delores starts to come to, "Oh, my goodness, where am I?"

"Delores, Delores, is that you I hear, I know that voice anywhere?"

"Yes, that's her, Gary," says Auntie Pam.

"Delores, come close to me so I can see you."

"It's not possible, he is dead, he died, it's not possible!"

Auntie Pam walks over to Delores and stands over top of her, "Yes, it is possible, you thought he was dead because you had him killed," yells Auntie Pam.

"What, wait, everybody, calm down; my mother would not have my father killed! I know she wasn't my best mother, but she wouldn't take away my daddy; she knew how much we loved each other."

"Terri, you need to know the truth about your no-good ass mother; your mother was incredibly angry about Gary not marrying her, and she would have done anything to destroy him and my family. She blames my mother for her father's death and she wanted to crush my family by having Gary killed, but what she didn't know was he didn't die. We faked the funeral, and the only people who knew he was alive were me and the doctors who saved his life."

Gary has become anxious, and his hand is shaking, "Delores, come over here, please. I want to see you," says Gary.

"Calm down, Gary; you don't need to see her."

Terri is upset. "Mama, say something. Say something to my Auntie, tell her you did not have him a shot."

Delores doesn't say anything.

Kamal tries to comfort Terri while she cries, "I think everyone should leave."

The doctors come out to get Terri and Kamal and walk to the back of the baby's room.

"I have some good news and some bad news," says the doctor.

Terri takes a deep breath, "Okay, give us the bad news first."

"No, give us the good news first," says Kamal.

"Your son is doing well; his skull is intact, and you'll be able to take him home within the next few days."

"That's great news," says Terri.

"It is. Now for the bad news: As he grows, you will have to watch him carefully. He's young now, so you may not see much, but as he grows, watch his motor skills, speech, and how fast he picks up on things. He may be a little behind other kids his age."

"Are you saying he will be retarded," asks Terri.

"I wouldn't say retarded, but he may have some learning issues."

Terri is visibly upset. "It doesn't matter. We can hire the best teachers and therapists; he will be okay, and we will be okay."

Kamal hugs Terri and consoles her.

"Yes, we will be okay."

Terri and Kamal walk into the room where their baby is, and Terri rubs his head, "We are going to be just fine, and you are a miracle."

Back out in the lobby, Delores is trying to get herself together, but Auntie Pam is making it difficult.

"You need to leave and crawl back into the hole you crawled out of," says Auntie Pam.

"I'm not going anywhere; I came for my daughter and my grandson!"

"If you don't leave this hospital right now, I'm going to have you arrested for the attempted murder of my brother!"

"Pam, calm down. Delores, please come close so I can see you; my eyesight is bad."

Delores looks at Pam and then around the room; she stands up and walks toward Gary.

Pam and Martin stand next to Gary's wheelchair along with his caregiver.

"Hello, Gary," Delores stutters.

Gary smiles, "Delores, you are still beautiful."

"Oh my God, he is obviously delusional," says Auntie Pam.

"Pam, shut the hell up and let me talk; I am not delusional."

Auntie Pam folds her arms, "he doesn't remember much now, and thank God for that, but he knew you were the one that put a hit on him."

Delores rolls her eyes at Pam, "Hi Gary, I'm so glad to see you." Tears rolled down her cheeks.

"Where is our baby Delores? Did you bring her with you?"

"His mind comes and goes because he has dementia," says his caregiver.

Delores takes a deep breath. "Gary, our baby is a big girl now." Delores wipes her tears.

"Her name is Terri, right?"

"Delores smiles, "Yes, her name is Terri; Delores reaches out to touch Gary's hand.

For The Sake of Love II

Auntie Pam smacks her hand, "No, don't touch him."

"Gary, where have you been? How come you stayed away so long."

"that's enough, take him back to the hotel, I can't play these games with this bitch."

"Look, Pam, I am not going to be your bitch, and I'm not going to stand here and take your smart-ass comments. You don't like me, and I can't stand you, now what? Do you want a piece of me, because I sure as hell want a piece of you?" Delores stands her ground.

Auntie Pam unfolds her arms, "Do you think I would stoop so low as to cause a scene in front of these people? You see," Pam laughs," that's the low-budget bitch you are."

Delores smacks Pam, "I got your low budget."

Delores clearly underestimated Pam because Pam lunged at her, and the two of them started fighting. There was so much commotion the nurses had to call security.

Terri and Kamal hear the commotion and see people running to the lobby. "What is going on out there? " Terri asks.

"I'll go see you stay with the baby," says Kamal.

Kamal runs out into the lobby and sees Delores and Pam being restrained by security.

"What the hell are you people doing? My son is in here bandaged from head to toe, and people are grieving. This young man's girlfriend was shot, and you two ladies are fighting!" Kamal is livid.

"If you don't know how to conduct yourselves, please leave because we need people to support us at this time. Terri doesn't need her family out here fighting."

"I came for my daughter and not to listen to this bitch disrespect me."

"No disrespect Ms. Delores, you seem to be the problem here so maybe you should go back to Ohio"

Pam gathers her composure, "Exactly, everyone Terri needs is here."

"Auntie Pam, no disrespect to you, but your niece doesn't need this right now," says Kamal.

"Well, alright, Kamal," Devonna whispers to Nina.

"Get off of me," says Auntie Pam.

The security guards let them both go.

"Kamal, I want to apologize to you and my niece because this is not me, and there is no excuse for my behavior."

"I need someone to take me to my daughter's house so I can recoup from this foolishness."

"The only place you're going to recoup is behind bars for the sale of baby and the hit for hire on my son."

"You're crazy, I never did such a thing, and you have no proof."

Auntie Pam whips out her cell phone and plays a recording of a conversation between Mrs. Phillips and Delores.

Delores hears the tape, "Stop, you can't prove that was me."

"I can't, but Mrs. Phillips can, and she will be more than happy to testify against you."

Terri heard everything, "Play the tape, Auntie Pam."

Auntie Pam plays the tape while Terri, Kamal, Kamal's family, Martin, Devonna, Nina, and the security officers listen.

Delores is motionless and drops her head. The thirty-minute conversation is definitely proof that Delores ordered a hit on Gary and sold Martin to the Phillips for money.

Terri walks toward her mother, but Kamal tries to stop her, "You are a hateful woman; there is no good in you. You had my father killed, and my baby was taken from me all because you were selfish. It wasn't because I was a teenager; no, you gave that woman my baby for the money and the connection to killing my father. That is you on tape asking her to kill my father!" Terri is furious.

"Wait, I can explain," says Delores. This is the dream she never wanted to come true.

"Explain; you want me to listen to you explain how you took the only person who loved me away from me. You made my life miserable, first my baby and then my father, I hate you, no I despise you, no, no, I pity you."

"I think we better leave," says Nina.

"Yeah, you're right," says Devonna.

The two of them scurry out of the hospital in shock at the events of the last 72 hours.

Delores cries, "I'm sorry, I'm so sorry."

"You're sorry things finally caught up to you," says Auntie Pam.

Martin walks over to Delores, "Why, why would you do that to your daughter."

"Because she wanted your father to be with DeeDee because she was prettier, and he was a Pastor's son. She ripped you from my arms as I cried out to her to bring you back because she didn't want me and Chauncey to be together. Isn't that right?"

Delores doesn't answer her.

"My father married my aunt?" Martin was confused.

"He married her, and they have two children together," says Terri.

"This is getting worse by the minute," Kamal takes his family down to catch a cab.

Auntie Pam, Delores, Terri, and Martin stood in the lobby.

"Tell my son how you plotted and planned for his father to marry his auntie because I wasn't pretty, isn't that what you said? A pastor's son needs a pretty wife; remember telling me that." Terri tried not to become emotional.

"Terri, it wasn't like that; I knew you could make it in the world," said Delores.

"I spent more than half of my life with a broken heart for my father and my son all because of you. I never want to see or hear from you ever again. I don't want you to go to prison; no, I want you to stay in Ohio with the one you love and adore. You see, everything you tried to destroy me with and take from me, I have it back."

Aunt Pam didn't like it. "Oh no, she's going to prison; I knew you were behind it, but I couldn't prove it until Mrs. Phillips sent me this tape a few days ago."

"Pam, this is all your fault," says Delores.

"Get the hell out of here, enough of you blaming everyone but yourself."

Delores grabs her suitcase and walks toward the elevator.

Terri walks behind her. "Wait, if you ever try to contact me again or come anywhere near me or my family, I promise you I will see to it you spend the rest of your life in prison."

Delores holds her head up high and steps onto the elevator, "So be it," the elevator closed.

Chapter Four

This is Goodbye

For The Sake of Love II

Delores stands on the curb in front of the hospital, tears streaming down her face as she looks around, feeling completely lost and overwhelmed. She is painfully aware of the terrible things she has done - ordering Gary's killing and selling Terri's baby.

Kamal walks up behind Delores, "Why did you do it?"

"Kamal, I was stupid, mad, and in love all at the same time, but Terri wants nothing to do with me now."

"Ms. Delores I believe in family and I want my son to have all the love from both sides of his family."

Tears from Delores, "How, you heard Terri, she wants me to stay away from her and her family. She's done with me."

Kamal hugs Delores, he feels sorry for her, "We will find a way to bring this family back together."

Delores doubts a family reunion will ever happen as she embraces Kamal.

For The Sake of Love II

2 months later.

The investigations start

Terri and Kamal brought their baby home from the hospital, and he is recovering and playing, and things seem normal with him.

Otischia came home from the hospital, but she's not one hundred percent; Martin is right by her side, along with her family and friends.

Auntie Pam agreed to let Terri and her father bond. Therefore, she let him stay in Boston with Terri and Kamal.

Terri hired staff to take care of her father around the clock, including Kamal's sister Carla. Big Gary doesn't remember much, but he is starting to remember that Terri is his daughter. Terri wants her father to walk her down the aisle, even if he is in a wheelchair.

Kamal's veterinarian hospital in the inner city is doing very well, and money is rolling in.

Terri wants to focus on her upcoming wedding but the police won't let her because they're investigating her car accident, and Otichia and Martin's attempted murder. The police have been asking questions and visiting off and on.

It's early morning and Terri has the same routine; she jumps out of bed, brushes her teeth, takes a quick shower, checks on the baby, and then goes to her father's bedroom to sit next to him. She quietly gazes into his face, and sometimes she reads a book, plays music, and sings to him.

Martin is the big man at Terri's Marketing firm now that everyone knows he is Terri's son, Terri let him take charge until she returns full time. Martin wants to make his mother proud so he is making all the right moves to keep his mother's marketing firm on top.

Delores returned to Ohio to find more problems were waiting for her because DeeDee moved her out of the mother-in-law's suite.

With nowhere to go and no friends, Delores moved into a senior building where she kept to herself.

The Wedding month,

Terri has been running around like a crazy woman trying to get everything perfect for the wedding, she is close to losing her mind.

The housekeeper knocks on Terri's bedroom door, "Ms. Dozier, your dress has arrived,"

"Oh my goodness I forgot all about my dress is coming today." Terri rushes to open her bedroom door.

The housekeeper hands her the dress bag, "here you are."

Terri's cell phone rings, "Hello,"

"Hey Terri I really need to talk to you, it's important," says Nina.

'I can't right now; I'm doing a million things for the wedding; it's going to have to wait."

Nina made it sound urgent, "It can't wait, Terri."

Terri becomes frustrated, "It will have to wait, Nina; damn, I'm getting married, my father is here, and I'm still breastfeeding, so tell me, what in the world could be more important than what I already have going on."

Before Nina can answer, Terri starts up again.

"I'm trying to maintain my weight, and that is killing me. You don't know how bad I would like to eat some Pepperidge Farm Bordeaux cookies, eat some crabs with my special sauce and drink a beer. I can't, so I'm cranky and nervous all at the same time."

Nina listens.

"Nina, are you there?"

"Yes, I'm here, and I'm not here to stress you out, but ….."

"Nina, it will have to wait until I am Mrs. Bodkin and back from my honeymoon before you load me down with stuff."

Nina remains silent.

"Nina, I'm sorry, I'm just a wreck; the past few months have been a roller coaster, and I just want to get off of it and have some sane time. You understand, right.?"

"I do, but I manage all of your finances, and when there are changes, I really need to make you aware of them."

"I know, I get it. Do what you need to do to handle it. I trust you. When all of this is done, we can sit down, and you can let me know the details."

"Okay,"

"As long as I'm not broke, I'm good."

Nina raises her left eyebrow, "okay."

Terri smiles, "Great! My dress just came, and I can't wait to see it. Did you, Otishcia, and Devonna get your dresses?"

"Yes, they called me, and they received theirs, and mine came yesterday, but I have to say I'm surprised you let Devonna be in your wedding."

"I couldn't have two bridesmaids, people would think I don't have friends," Terri laughs, no I'm just joking, I like Devonna you know that. We fuss and curse each other out, but she's real and I love real."

Nina sighs, "Okay, I'll let you get back to your wedding and I'll see you at the bridal shower."

"Okay talk to you later."

"Wait what about your sister?"

It was too late Terri had already hung up.

"I've got to tell her what is going on and when I do, the shit is going to hit the fan. I can't believe Kamal

For The Sake of Love II

would do this to her." Nina doesn't want to delay the news until her best friend is married.

"I am going to be a beautiful bride," Terri's eyes lit up at the sight of her wedding gown. Her long floor-length lavender silk dress, off the shoulders to show off her boobs and a tight middle section. "Kamal is going to love me in this."

Kamal knocks on her dressing room door, "Babe are you in there."

Terri rushes to put the dress up, "Wait a minute, honey, I'll be right out."

"What are you doing, can I come in?"

"Noooooo, you cannot, I said I'll be right out."

Kamal heard her this time; her tone was definitely noticeable.

Terri opens the door. "Okay, hi, honey." Terri smiles and kisses him on the lips.

"Wow, that kiss totally took me by surprise, especially considering how you were sounding just a few moments ago!"

Terri cut straight to the chase, her tone unapologetic. "Look, I was in the middle of something, and your interruptions were a bit much."

"Look, Ms. Dozier, I am practically your husband, and you don't have anything I haven't seen."

"Awwww, but I do." Terri laughs.

They both laugh.

"So the word on the street is you're getting ready to marry a handsome young man from Trinidad."

"Oh really, well, they are lying on the street."

"So you're not getting married to a handsome young man from Trinidad."

"Nope," Terri holds back her laugh but she is about to burst inside.

Kamal looks at Terri seriously, "Terri, what's up? You're calling the wedding off."

"No, silly, but I'm not marrying a young man; he's handsome, yes, and from Trinidad, yes, but you left out sexy."

Kamal places his hands on his side. " Oh, I get it. You're saying I'm an old man."

Terri starts walking toward the dining room area, "you got it."

"Aww man, that's cold Terri."

They start laughing again, Kamal grabs Terri from behind around her waist, "Can an old man fuck you as I fuck you?" Kamal immediately thinks about Rob. "Never mind don't answer that."

Terri turns to face him, "Why not,"

"You need me to say it?"

"Yeah, say it." Terri is curious

"I thought about old man Rob fucking you."

Terri has a blank look on her face, "okay," she turns around and continues walking into the dining room.

"I know I shouldn't be thinking about him because I'm the one you're marrying."

"Exactly, but I can see why it came to your mind, I'm not mad."

Kamal changed the subject, "How was your afternoon? Was the baby good?"

Terri's face lights up. " He was perfect. He is growing and doing so well. I just love his cute face and his chubby body."

"I do too, have you thought about your mother?"

Terri's smile is replaced by a scowling look, her eyebrows go down, and her lips protrude, "Are you trying to fuck up the rest of my day, dude."

"No, I'm not, but I promised her I would work on you letting her come to the wedding."

"I'm not hearing you right. I know you didn't just say anything about me and my mother, no scratch that, that lady working on anything. Kamal, are we a team or not, honey? I need to know now."

Kamal places his hand on top of Terri's hand, "Babe, we are a family."

Terri snatches her hand away from Kamal's, "fuck her and fuck whoever associates with her, the lady has no heart. You were there, you heard my Auntie Pam; you know what? I'm not having this conversation with you."

Terri turns to walk to the kitchen to get a salad out of the refrigerator.

When she closes the refrigerator, Kamal stands in her personal space. "I love you, and I want our son to have a complete family with no drama. I don't want to answer any questions when he becomes a man and asks you and me about his Nana."

"We'll tell him the truth; she died."

Terri sits at the kitchen table, stuffing a salad into her mouth.

There's a knock at the door, and it's Martin.

Martin rushes into the house after Victoria, the housekeeper, lets him in, "Where's my mother?"

"I believe she's in the kitchen."

"Terri, Terri!"

"Oh my God, is that Martin? Something must be wrong." Terri jumps up from the table and walks toward him. "What's wrong?"

Martin is noticeably upset, "My father, he's dead."

"Chauncey or Mr. Phillips?"

"My real dad is dead!"

"Okay, wait, I'm confused; Chauncey is dead," asks Terri.

"Mom, yes, I told you already."

That was the very first time Martin had ever called Terri Mom.

Terri grabs him and hugs him while Kamal stands back, feeling left out.

"Come over here and sit," says Terri.

Kamal looks at Terri, "Are you okay? He told you already."

"I must have forgotten, my memory hasn't been right since the car accident."

"I checked my phone messages and he left me a message two months ago."

"You're just checking your messages," asks Kamal.

Terri and Martin turn and look at Kamal.

"What, I'm asking, he left him a message two months ago."

"A lot was going on and I was busy dodging bullets, taking care of my girl and my mother, and finding out my grandfather is alive, so excuse me for not thinking about messages on my phone."

Terri feels the tension, "okay, everyone calm down."

"I am calm," says Kamal, but he's really mad that Martin has authority in his voice. He feels like Martin is trying his manhood.

Terri looks at Kamal and nods her head and Kamal leaves the room.

"Okay, honey tell me what's happening."

The housekeeper brings Martin a glass of Iced Tea.

"Thank you," says Martin, "I got his message that he wanted to talk to me about what he knows about me and he told me to give him a call, but you know I didn't have time with everything going on around here. I called him today, and it was a message," Kamal takes out his phone and dials the phone number so Terri can hear the message, "Hi this is Chauncey's daughter, and we regret to inform you that our father is deceased if you have any questions you can call 555-6029 and speak to one of his daughters."

Terri grabs her chest, "Oh my God, Chauncey is dead."

"I googled his name, and the news article said he was murdered in his driveway; I'm freaking out because I was shot at in the driveway, and he died the day before I was shot at. Somebody was trying to kill him, me, and you."

Terri becomes worried, "Kamal, Kamal, come here!"

Kamal rushes to her, "What's wrong?"

Terri is hyperventilating, "Chauncey was murdered the same day I had the car accident and the day before Martin and Otichia were shot at. Baby, this was a hit; someone was trying to kill us."

"But why," ask Kamal?"

Terri looks at Martin, "I don't know, but I know who does know."

"Who," asks Kamal and Martin at the same time.

'My Goddam mother, I'm going to Ohio to see DeeDee and Delores and find out what is going on."

"Oh no, you're not. Our baby needs you, and we are getting married in two weeks. This can wait."

"Honey, my son's father was murdered. He needs, or we need answers."

Kamal wants to calm himself before he says something that could change everything, "Terri, please wait until after the wedding; you should be concentrating on your big day, and I'm sure your oldest son can wait until his mother is happily married." Kamal looks over at Martin.

At this moment, Terri has a choice: the man she loves or the son she has missed out on. Who will she choose?

"You're right; I need to stay focused on the wedding," she looks over at Martin. But as soon as we're back from the honeymoon, you and I will go to Ohio and find out what is happening."

Kamal sticks his chest out and looks at Martin, "You selfish bastard," he thinks to himself.

Martin rolls his eyes, "I'll get a flight out tomorrow and see what I can find out."

Kamal sees what Martin is trying to do; he wants Terri to feel guilty.

"I will get you a private flight there," she says, walking over to her purse. She then takes my credit card and books his hotel and car.

Martin looks at Kamal and Terri and says, "I don't need your money; I need your support."

Martin walks away and to his car.

Terri runs behind him, "Look at me. You have my support, but I need you to be reasonable and not irrational. Let's do this together when I get back. Don't make this about you or me. You and I are a team, and no one, do you hear me, will ever come between that."

Martin looks over at Kamal standing in the doorway.

"Okay, Mom,"

The two of them hug, and Terri is all smiles. Hearing her son call her mom lights up her inner being. "That's my son."

Terri stands in the driveway as Martin drives away; when she can no longer see his car, she turns around and walks into the house.

Kamal is sitting in the living room having a glass of wine when she walks over to him, leans over, and kisses his cheek.

"Come have a seat next to me," says Kamal.

"I can't. I hear the baby crying, and I need to check on my dad."

"Dammit, Terri, I am your husband, and I need some of your time. Ever since your father came to stay and your son came into your life, you don't have time for me."

"Wait, weren't you the one that said less than an hour ago that family is important and how you want me to bond with my mother? Well, I'm bonding with my son, whom I haven't seen in thirty-seven years. I thought my father was dead for most of my life, Kamal, and now I have a short time to love on him, and I want to cherish every moment."

"What about you and me," asked Kamal.

"What about us? We are about to be married and spend the rest of our lives together. Why are you acting like this?" Terri is confused.

"I don't know. I feel like I'm being eased out of my space."

Terri places arms around her man, "I don't know about easing out but I got something you can ease into."

Kamal chuckles, "That sounds nice,"

The Nanny interrupts them, "Ms. Terri, the baby needs milk!"

"Oh, I gotta go feed the baby; he needs me if that's okay with you."

"Yeah, well, at least he's getting what he needs."

Terri waves her hand, "I can't make everybody happy, Goddammit."

Kamal decides to leave and go to a bar in the city.

Terri sits in the nursery holding the baby and listening to soothing music while she feeds him.

Hours later, and Kamal still isn't back, Terri decides to spend time with her father. Even though it's late, he's up, and the two of them play cards together. Terri feels like a little girl spending time with her dad, even though she knows tomorrow he might not remember her name.

For The Sake of Love II

In Ohio,

Martin has arrived in Ohio

He hasn't spoken with his adoptive parents since he left Ohio two months ago, but since he's in Ohio, he decided to pay them both a visit.

When he pulled up to his parents' home, he could tell something was wrong because the front yard looked unkept. His parents always made sure the lawn was kept up with blooming flowers and perfectly manicured grass. He still had his door key, so he tried to use it, but it didn't work. " What is going on around here?" He walked to the back of the house, and it was worse than the front. The pool was dirty, and the patio was literally a mess.

Martin calls his mother, but there is no answer; he then tries his father's cell phone.

"Hello," answers Mr. Phillips.

Martin started in, "Dad, I'm at the house, and my key doesn't fit. Mom is not answering the phone, and the house looks bad."

"Son, calm down. Your mother had a heart attack, and she's in a nursing home, and I'm in Washington with my.." Mr. Phillips didn't want to say anything more.

"Wait a minute. Mom is sick, and no one called me. Why didn't someone contact me?" Martin was concerned.

"I figured you were busy in Boston with your new job."

"Dad, she is my mother; I would have stopped everything for her."

"Are you sure about that?"

"What do you mean am I sure about that, dam right I'm sure," says Martin.

Mr. Phillips wants to tell Martin he knows everything, but he doesn't want to do it over the phone. " How long will you be in Ohio?"

"I came to find out what happened to my fa," Martin realizes he slipped.

"I'll be there in the morning; meet me at the house around ten o'clock."

"Have you seen the house? It looks horrible on the outside; it looks like a ghost mansion."

"I am putting it up for sale real soon."

"Where will you and mom live?"

"We'll talk about that tomorrow, son."

"Where is mom? I want to go see her."

"We'll go tomorrow and visit her together."

"Okay, I'll see you tomorrow, Dad."

Martin senses something is not right, and his father doesn't sound like everything is good with his mother.

Martin walks back to his car and calls Chauncey's number again. Once again, his daughter's recording comes on with a number to reach her. Martin writes down the number.

"How can I introduce myself to them?"

"Hello,"

Martin hesitates, "Hel-lo"

"Hello,"

"Hi, I'm sorry, my name is Martin Phillips, and I know your father; I called him, and I got your message."

"Yes, how can I help you," asks Channel.

Martin is nervous, he starts sweating under his armpits, "First, I'm sorry for your loss."

"Thank you. What did you say your name was again?"

"Martin, Martin Phillips."

"Oh, okay, I heard him talking about you recently."

"You did," Martin is surprised.

"Yes, I'm pretty sure I did; he told me and my older sister that he had a son named Martin."

"He did!"

"Yes, he did. We asked questions, but he didn't tell us much more than that."

"If you don't mind, can we meet up and talk?"

"I don't know you, no I'm not meeting a stranger."

"I completely understand, I'm sorry."

"What about a zoom call, can we do it that way?"

"I tell you what because we are just as curious as you are, "let's meet out and like at a Panera Bread."

Martin is excited, "That sounds great, when?"

"The day after tomorrow, around eleven o'clock, my sister and I will meet you."

"Okay, I can't wait; please lock in my number in case something comes up. You can call me."

"Okay, bye." Channel hangs up.

Martin smiles, "I'm glad I came; now I can get to the bottom of a lot of stuff, like who would want to see me dead."

Martin went and checked into a hotel near his family home; once he was all checked in, it was hard for him to relax, "who would kill Chauncey, shoot at me, and run into Terri's car? Something is not adding up."

Terri calls, "Hey baby, are you settled in? Did you see your mother? I mean, Mrs. Phillips."

"No, apparently, I've missed a lot here; my mother is in a nursing home; she had a heart attack, and the house is locked up; my father is coming from DC tomorrow so that we can talk."

"Please be careful because if you think someone has it out for us, you need to be very careful."

For The Sake of Love II

"Guess what, I am meeting Chauncey's daughters in two days. I spoke with them, and they agreed to meet with me."

Terri is surprised, "They are your sisters and your cousins."

"Hey, you're right, their mother is your big sister."

"Yes, she is my big sister." The thought of DeeDee made her skin crawl.

"It's a lot I don't know about my real family; some days, I'm confused about who I am."

"I know, but hopefully, it will all come together soon."

"Where is Kamal," asks Martin.

"He left after you left."

"Can I say something,"

"Sure, what is it? You can say or ask me anything."

"Are you sure he's the one for you?"

Terri wasn't expecting that question. " Yes, I'm sure. Kamal loves me, and I love him. We have been through some crazy stuff, but I believe he loves me."

"It takes more than love to make a relationship work, it takes understanding, commitment, and patience."

"Well, aren't you the expert on love? I believe we have all of that. I have been busy with the baby, my father, and you, and he feels neglected, that's all."

"That's my point; he shouldn't feel that way. You just got your father and son back into your life. It's a big deal, and he's being selfish to me."

"You let me handle Kamal. Now get some rest, and we'll talk tomorrow."

Terri hangs the phone up, "he's right, a lot has changed in my life; at first, it was me and the dog; now, it's me, a baby, a grown son, an elderly father, and the dog. Speaking of Zoey, where is she"

Terri calls for Zoey.

For The Sake of Love II

The next day,

Martin showers and prepares to meet with his father. He grabs a pair of blue jeans out of his suitcase and a tan cotton button-down shirt. He has so much running through his brain, like, "Do you know you're not my biological father? How do I tell him he's not my dad? What did his wife do? This is going to be a lot to deal with today."

Martin arrived at the house and saw his father's car in the driveway. He was nervous, and it showed on his face.

Martin gets out of the car and sees people cleaning the house and taking care of the lawn. His father walks out to greet him.

"Hey son," they both hug.

"Hey Dad, how have you been; how is Washington treating you?"

"You know, son, it's the same bullshit, Congress won't pass the gun reform, and meanwhile, the white terrorist groups are shooting up schools, and the black gangs are shooting up the neighborhoods. It's a mess, but enough about me, what have you been up to up there in Boston?"

Martin breathes deep. "Well, Dad, that's why I'm here. A lot has happened, and I want to talk to you about it."

"Okay, come into my office while Jonae' makes us something to eat."

"Let's talk in the living room; it's less business and more personal," says Martin.

"Okay," the two of them walk into the living room; Mr. Phillips is walking slowly because of his bad hip and bad knees.

"Why is my mom in a nursing home?"

"She had a bad fall, and umm, I felt that it would be best to put her there."

"Why can't she move to DC and be with you, or can you come home more often to be with her?"

Mr. Phillips is becoming uncomfortable with Martin's questions: "Well, son, a lot is going on, and your mother isn't well. She's up in age and she's sick. I can't take care of her; she needs 24-hour care, and I put her in the best nursing facility."

Martin nods his head, "Okay, I see." Martin leans forward and places his hands together; his palms are sweaty. I found out something about Mom and a lady who used to work for you named Delores."

"Yes, I remember Delores, she was my paralegal."

"She had two daughters that were teenagers at the time she was working for you and, and, and one of them had a baby, a baby boy, and what I'm trying to say is," Martin is emotional, "I'm the boy she had, my real mother's name is Terri, and my father's name is Chauncey, they met in high school."

Mr. Phillips is noticeably calm a little too calm for Martin.

"Dad, did you just hear what I said?"

"Yes son, I heard you, and you're not telling me anything I didn't already know."

Martin jumps up, "What! You knew, for how long?"

"Since you were a young boy, but I didn't know who your father was."

"But you knew Delores's daughter was my mother?" Martin paces the floor

"Son, calm down,"

"No, I will not calm down. You and Mom kept this from me, and all the time, I'm clueless."

"Your mother wanted a child, and she did what she did to make me happy,"

"So you know the story, you know everything."

"Yes, but I didn't know who your real father was, and I didn't know you were Delores's grandson right away."

"Oh my God, you guys have been lying to me all these years."

"I loved you, gave you all that I had, and left you in my Will. I look at you as my son."

"Even though I'm not."

"Yes, I raised you, and you are a Phillips."

"Mom didn't want this to get out because she said it would ruin your political career."

"No, your mom didn't want this to get out because it would ruin me and her. How can raising a child that's not yours ruin my career? Please, I would have been considered a hero in the eyes of the people. Your mother was selfish and did it to keep me married to her."

"I can't believe this, and now my biological father was murdered in his driveway; who would want him dead?"

"Your mother," says Mr. Phillips.

Martin was in shock, "Mom had him killed!"

"Yes, he was getting close to finding you, and she wanted to stop him. She would have stopped anyone who had exposed the truth."

"Wait a minute dad, I was shot two months ago coming out of my house with my girlfriend, my girlfriend almost died, did mom do that too."

Mr. Phillips doesn't answer him.

"She did that to me, she wanted to silence me too?"

Mr. Phillips nods his head.

"Oh my God she is sick, wait Terri was in an accident a car rammed her car, please tell me."

"It was your mother, she had all of you targeted to keep the truth from me."

For The Sake of Love II

"She wanted to kill us to prevent you from knowing something you already knew?"

"Yep," Mr. Phillips shook his head.

"What else has she done?"

"She kidnapped Delores and had her held up in the basement of this house and blackmailed her about the murder for hire."

"Ohhhhh, now I see; that's what Terri was talking about when her father showed up."

"What, what are you saying, he's not dead."

"Oh, you don't know, he's alive, he's old as hell, but he's alive."

"Does Delores know he's alive?"

"Yes, she was there at the hospital and saw him with her own eyes."

Mr. Phillips laughs, "I know she wanted to pee herself."

Martin laughs too, and then he looks serious, "Is mom going to prison?"

"She needs to, but no, son. I put her in a nursing home, and she'll stay there until, well, until."

"What about you?"

"Sit down, son,"

"Oh no, what are you going to tell me."

For The Sake of Love II

"This is difficult but I hope you don't judge me; I have two daughters with a woman that I have been with for the past forty years."

"No, no, pops, no, you have other children?"

"Yes, and I told your mother, and that is what gave her the heart attack."

"This is getting crazier by the minute."

For The Sake of Love II

Chapter Five

Let's meet the Family.

Martin and Mr. Phillips spent hours talking about his childhood, and now Martin feels even more confused than before. Not only does he have two sisters that he's never met from his biological father, but he also has siblings from his foster father that he has never met.

Now Martin has taken on the task of telling his sisters from his biological father that he is their brother, and he is uncertain how things will go.

The next day

Once again, Martin wakes up with his nerves on edge. Lately, it seems that every day is an adventure and something new. He decided to dress down a little by wearing ripped blue Levi's jeans, a green T-shirt, and a thick gold chain around his neck.

Martin pulls up at Panera Bread, but he doesn't know what they look like, so he doesn't know if they are there or not. His cell phone rings a few seconds after he pulls up.

"Hi, this is Channel. We are already here. Did you just pull up in a white car?"

"Yes, I just pulled up."

"Okay, I'll come to the door." Channel walks over to the door, opens it, and waves at Martin.

Martin smiles; he's excited but nervous at the same time.

As soon as Martin saw them, he was relieved to see a resemblance; he wondered why he looked different from his parents and other family members all of his life.

"Hi, I'm Martin Phillips," he extends his hand for a handshake, but Channel opens her arms for a hug. Martin wasn't expecting that.

Chandra hugs him too,

Martin was starting to relax.

"Would you like something to eat," asks Martin.

"Sure, we were going to order, but we didn't know what type of meeting this was," Channel says. How do you know my father?

Martin started to get nervous again, "Should I just say it?" he asked himself.

They notice his awkward, blank stare into space. "Hello, why did you ask us to meet you here?"

"I am your father's son," Martin bursts out. "I mean, we have the same father."

"We kind of figured that out; you look just like him."

Martin is surprised, "What do you mean,"

"Okay, our father told us before he died, like two years ago, that he had a son, but he didn't know where he was, but he knew his name, and he told us he was looking for you."

"Whew, I was worried about meeting you two today."

"What was he like? Tell me about him. I want to know everything, and maybe talking about him will help you, but if it's too much, I understand," Martin rambles on.

Chandra starts to cry. "I miss him so much. He was kind, and he spoiled us to death."

Martin walks over to get some napkins.

"That's what my, I mean, our father, would have done; he was thoughtful and kind. Our grandfather was a Pastor, so my father was all about kindness."

"Wow, I see myself in you two."

"Yep, you look like our father; here is a picture of him," Chandra pulls out her cell phone and shows him a picture.

Martin looks at the picture and becomes emotional. "Wow,"

"Who is your mother," asked Chandra

"Wait, he didn't tell you my mother's name."

"No, he just said he had a child when he was very young, and the girl was young too."

Martin doesn't know if he should say something or not, "so he said he had a son but never told you who the mother was?"

Channel hunches her shoulders, "I mean, what's the big deal? It's not like we know her; we weren't even born yet."

"Let's get something to eat; I'm hungry," Martin wants to get off of the subject."

"Did you find your mother," asks Channel.

"Slow down, let's get something to eat, and then we can talk more," Martin says. He pulls out his wallet, and the three of them walk up to order food and drinks.

"It's nice having a big brother," says Channel.

"Why so he can buy you things; you're just like mom, a freeloader."

Channel is offended, "I'm not a freeloader; I just like having a big brother."

"Please Channel, you've only had a big brother for twenty-four hours."

Martin laughs, "Is this what it's like having little sisters?"

Channel and Chandra laugh, "I guess so."

The food is on the table, and they start eating; Martin has a hefty appetite.

"I wonder if grandma and granddad know about you," asks Channel.

"I don't know who knows about me."

"Well, there are a lot of us, so you have a lot of family on Dad's side," says Chandra.

"That's good because I've lived as an only child all of my life."

"Well you're no longer an only child because you have us," says Chandra.

"I googled you," says Chandra, "and I know where you live, work, and basically everything else. I know you've never been to jail; your credit is good and you live in Boston. That's where our auntie Terri lives. She is so cool. She and my mom don't get along but we love her. She sends us gifts, but we don't tell Mom. She's rich, and I mean really rich, like a rich bitch."

"Okay that's enough, don't call her a bitch," says Channel.

Chandra continues talking and eating, "Her and our mom don't get along, I think it started when they were children."

"Did your mother ever say what happened," asked Martin

"Mom says Auntie Terri was jealous of her because she is prettier than she is."

"Is she prettier than your aunt?"

"Oh yes, our mother is beautiful; that's why dad fell for her," says Chandra.

"But Auntie Terri has the brains; she owns her own marketing firm, and she graduated top of her class; she has traveled around the world," says Channel

"She got that money from her dad; his family was wealthy and powerful in Ohio," says Chandra.

"I don't care. When I finish college, I'm going to live with Aunt Terri and work for her," says Channel.

"How many more years until you finish," asks Martin.

"This is my last year, and then I'm done," says Chandra.

"I graduate with my doctorate this year," says Channel.

"Wow, you ladies are smart, I'm impressed."

Martin managed to make them forget about his mother, but he got all the information he needed to make his next move.

"I want to meet my grandparents," says Martin.

"Okay, we can take you to meet them. They are old, very old, but I think you should still meet them," says Chandra

"How about we go to their church on Sunday if you're still in town," says Channel.

"Perfect. I'll still be in town." Martin's cell phone rings, and it's Terri. Excuse me, I need to take this call."

Martin steps away from the table, "hello,"

"Hello, how are things going there? The wedding is days away. Are you coming back?"

"Yes, I am sitting here with my sisters, and they are telling me all about my dad and my grandparents, and they even talked about you."

"Me, what did they say?"

"You are the best auntie in the world."

Terri laughs, "Is that so? Why? Because I send gifts and money to the college."

"No, because you're smart. I'm going to meet my father's parents on Sunday, and I'll fly back right after that."

"Okay, but I must tell you, my nieces don't know I'm your mother."

"I kind of figured that out."

"I don't know how that will go, but I'm here if you need me."

"Thank you, mom,"

Terri becomes emotional.

Martin reacts to the silence, "Hey, are you still there?"

"Yes, baby, I'm here; I was thinking about the years I missed hearing you call me MOM,"

"I have to go. They're waiting for me in the restaurant. I'll call you when I leave."

Martin returns to the table, "Sorry about that, it was my mother."

"Oh yeah, who is your biological mother," asks Channel.

Martin dodges answering them, "We can discuss her later; I need to take care of some things before Sunday."

They all get up from the table; Martin walks them to their car, "Nice car."

"It belongs to our mom, but she let us drive it when we are home from college.

Martin thinks to himself, "Blue Tesla, hmmm. " He remembers the car from somewhere but can't place it just yet.

Martin drives to the facility his adopted mother is and he thinks of how he is going to tell his sisters that he's Terri's son.

Martin pulls up at the nursing home and looks around the grounds as he pulls up. He admires the lawn, flowers, and the way the place looks. He walks in and is escorted to the recreation area' he sees his mother sitting in a chair slumped over, her head hanging to the left, and her silver-gray hair swept back into a ponytail. He walks over to her, "Mom," he starts crying.

Mrs. Phillips looks up at him. She can barely talk, but she can smile at him.

After hearing all the awful things she did to everyone to keep her secret, Martin still found love in his heart for her; after all, she gave him a good life. Martin touched her hair; he always loved how sleek she kept her hair. "I see you're wearing your favorite hairstyle."

Mrs. Phillips nods her head and smiles.

Martin kneels, "I spoke with Dad yesterday at the house,"

Mrs. Phillips turns her head, and an angry look comes over her face.

"He told me everything about him, you, and everybody involved in my existence. He knew all the time I wasn't his son, and yet he loved me anyway, and he must have loved you enough not to say anything."

Mrs. Phillips turns to Martin, "He didn't love me; he just married me." Her voice is low, and she speaks slowly, but Martin hears every word she says.

"I'm sorry you felt you needed to do all that to keep him."

Mrs. Phillips puts her hand on Martin's face. "I'm so sorry to hurt you and everybody. Please forgive me, son."

Tears roll down Mrs. Phillips's wrinkled, baby-soft face and she touches a soft spot in Martin.

"I forgive you, and I love you."

Martin leans his head toward her, and their foreheads touch, just as they used to do when he was a little boy after he had fallen off his bike or gotten hurt playing. They share a quiet moment as if the world had stopped and they were the only two existing.

Martin felt the life leave his mother, "Mom, mom, help, she's not breathing!" Martin jumps up and yells for a nurse, "Help,"

A nurse runs into the activity room and checks for a pulse, but there is no pulse. "I'm sorry, sir. You will have to leave."

"I'm not leaving," Martin is hysterical.

"Sir, I'm sorry your mother is dead."

Martin screams, "Noooooooooooooo!"

Martin calls his father, "Dad, she's dead, she died in my arms.!"

"Martin, calm down; who died in your arms?"

"Mom, I came to the nursing home to see her, and she died while I was here," Martin can't pull himself together.

"I'll catch a flight out in an hour and come to you, are you okay?"

"No, she died, she told me she was sorry, and then she took her last breath."

"Son, I know it's hard but your mother had a lot of health issues."

"You let her die in here; you didn't love her."

Mr. Phillips listens; he doesn't say anything."

"She loved me. While you were away all the time with your other family, she was the one taking care of me."

"Son, listen to me; she is also the same woman who just a few months ago tried to have you killed, your biological mother killed, and your biological father is dead because of her selfishness. So don't go crying all over the place for a woman as ruthless as her."

Martin hangs up the phone and leaves the nursing home, driving fast and out of control; he screams, "AHHHHHHHHHHHHHHHHHHHHHHHHHHHH HHHHHHHHHH!" he pulls the car over and calls Otishcia.

"Hello, babe, my mother just died."

"What? Terri is dead!"

"No, I'm sorry, my adopted mother."

"Whew, you scared me," she can hear how upset he is.

"I can come and be with you if you like."

"You would do that for me," Martin is surprised because all of his past girlfriends were self-absorbed.

"Don't be silly. That's your mom, and we're supposed to be there for each other; you're my man, dude."

Martin smiles and chuckles, "Thanks,"

"I got you to smile,."

They both laugh.

"Let me make some arrangements here, and I can be on a flight tomorrow."

"I'll ask Terri to let you use her plane, and maybe she'll come with you."

For The Sake of Love II

"No, I don't want to bother her. I don't ask Terri for anything, and I'm not about to start. Besides, she is planning her wedding. I'll book a flight out."

"Okay, call me with the details so I can pick you up," I love you."

"I love you too, babe."

Ever since the shooting, the two of them have gotten a lot closer, and the age difference is not a factor

Martin is back at the hotel when his father calls, "Hello."

"Son, we need to talk and plan your mother's funeral,"

I can't talk about this right now; I still need some time to process all of this; she died right in front of me."

"I understand; I'll be at the house until all is settled."

Martin hangs up and calls Terri, "Hello, Terri."

"Hey, Martin, how is everything in Ohio?"

"My mother died,"

"What, she died, when, what happened!"

"I went to visit her in the nursing home and," he sighs, "It's a long story. Anyway, Otishcia is coming tomorrow to be with me."

Martin is waiting for Terri to offer to come.

"That's great; you want to be alone; don't worry about the office. I'll pop in and check on things."

"Okay, I'll talk to you later."

Terri senses something is wrong, "If you need me to come, I will, but I have my dad, the baby, and the wedding coming up, so I can't stay long."

Martin was happy to know that Terri offered to come.

"Oh no, things will be fine, but I would like for you to come to the funeral."

"Martin, I haven't set foot in Ohio since I left for college and I haven't seen Mrs. Phillips since I was thirteen years old. I had no idea she had my baby all those years. I'm going to need a minute to think."

"I understand; there's a call coming in from my sisters; hold on."

"No you go ahead and call me back; I love you and if you need anything let me know."

Martin clicks over, "hello."

"Hey were you busy, we were wondering if you would like to hang out tonight."

"No, my adopted mother just died so I need to clear my head, but I'll take a rain check."

"We don't want you to be alone so why don't you come over here and hang out or we'll come to you."

"But what about your mother she doesn't know about me."

"You're our brother and it's time we let everyone know that," says Channel.

"you're the feisty one I see."

For The Sake of Love II

"Channel laughs, "Everyone says that."

"I'll take a raincheck besides I'm too old to hang out with you two."

Channel smirks, "please I'm twenty-four and she's twenty-two, why can't we hang with you?"

"He's right, he's going to look like an old man with us," says Chandra.

"We'll have to tell our mother about you, she probably knows already anyway. Our parents had a great relationship."

Chandra jumps right in to set the record straight, "That's a lie, if it was so great, why did he leave her with no money. He cut off our cell phones and he filed for divorce."

Martin is shocked, "Wow, all of that happened, why what changed?"

"I don't know, but I think it's time we took you around the family so you can meet them; if you're free Sunday, we can go to our grandfather's church," says Channel

"Okay, I'll be here for that.

Sunday morning

Once Otishcia landed, Martin forgot about going to church. He was busy showing her around where he grew up and the house he grew up in.

It's 8 am and Martin's cell phone rings, it's his sister, Channel

"Good morning," Martin's voice is groggy.

"Are you still in bed, get up we have to be in church at 9:30 and I don't want you to be late?"

Martin starts laughing, "Is this what having a little sister is like, bossy."

Otichia wakes up, "Who are you talking to?"

"It's my little sister Channel."

"Who is that," asks Chanel?

"It's my girlfriend."

Otishcia corrects Martin, "Excuse you, I'm past girlfriend dude."

Martin laughs, "you two are giving me the blues, let me get up and get dressed. I'll be there text me the address."

"Bring her too, so we can meet her."

Martin laughs, "This girl is too much, and she's bossy."

Otishcia looks at Martin, grinning and laughing. "You look happy. Actually, I haven't seen you this happy since I met you."

"I feel like I belong, and somebody wants me to be a part of them."

"What about Terri, she loves you."

"I know, but she's getting married, and she just had a new baby, so she's occupied with a lot right now. Come on get up and get dressed because we're going to church to meet the family."

Otishcia lays back in the bed and throws the covers off of her, exposing her naked body; she spreads her legs open and up in the air, "Are you sure you don't want to get back in this bed?"

"Girlllllllll, you are the devil tempting me," Martin shakes his head. I can't resist you; this is how Adam went down."

"Now you go down."

And that's just what Martin does, he went down and gave Otichia the thrill and chills she wanted."

After pleasing his woman his mind was back on church, "Okay, I'm going to church," Martin hops into the shower.

"Oh no, this is not over," Otichia says as she steps into the shower. As the water beats her face, she lowers herself down to return the favor to Martin.

Martin groans with the same ecstasy she did, and it doesn't take long for him to reach a climax.

Welcome to church

Channel turned around to look at the church doors ten times in ten seconds.

Martin and Otishcia show up at church a few minutes late.

Channel whispers and waves her hand. She saves them a seat next to her. " Hey, you two are late."

"Sorry, things kept coming up," says Martin.

Chandra taps Martin on the shoulder, "Hello."

DeeDee is sitting next to Chandra, "who is that?"

"It's our brother," says Chandra politely.

DeeDee can barely hold her composure. She starts moving in her seat and looking around. " He is who; you don't have a brother."

Chandra whispers, "Shhh, the Pastor started."

"Don't shhh me, you don't have a brother!"

DeeDee is the focus of the entire congregation, all eyes are on her.

"Excuse me is there a problem," asks the Pastor.

DeeDee jumps up, leaves out of the church, and goes to her car; she starts beating on the stirring wheel.

"This is a nightmare," DeeDee drives off.

After church, Channel and Chandra introduced Martin to the family, including uncles, aunts, and grandparents. Everyone was happy to meet him, and to

Martin's surprise, Chauncey had told his parents about him.

Martin was on top of the world. He and Otishcia were invited back to his grandparents' home for brunch and dinner. When Martin saw the big house they lived in and the beautiful grounds, he was at a loss for words.

"This is why I don't go to church," says Otishcia.

Martin looks at her, confused, "why?"

She lowers her voice. "Look around. They are taking money from the congregation to pay for this lavish lifestyle."

Martin is introduced to the whole family.

Meanwhile, DeeDee is upset that Martin showed up in her and her daughter's lives. She makes a call but does not get an answer, so she decides to drive over to Mr. Phillip's house. She walks up to the door and rings the bell and the housekeeper answers.

"Is Mrs. Phillips available?"

"Excuse me, ma'am. Mrs. Phillips is no longer with us."

Dee Dee's temper causes her to be rude to the housekeeper. "What do you mean she's no longer with us? Where is she? I need to talk with her."

The housekeeper decides to match DeeDee's rudeness, "I said she's not here," she closes the door.

DeeDee bangs on the door.

For The Sake of Love II

This time, Mr. Phillips answers the door, "Yes, how can I help you."

DeeDee pulled herself together quickly. She always respected Mr. Phillips and looked up to him. Clearing her throat, she said, "Hi, Mr. Phillips. I wasn't expecting you to answer the door."

"Clearly, what do you want?"

"I don't know if you remember me. I'm Delores's daughter, DeeDee. It's been a long time since you saw me and my sister Terri." DeeDee smiles.

Mr. Phillips hesitates and then opens the door, "come on in."

DeeDee glances around, looking for Mrs. Phillips

"What do you want," asked Mr. Phillips

"I'm looking for your wife, I need to speak with her regarding some business."

"What type of business did you have with my wife, she was an elderly woman with a lot of health problems."

"Wait, did you just say was an elderly woman?"

"Yes, was," Mr. Phillips walks slowly over to the bar and pours two glasses of brandy.

DeeDee follows behind him, "What happened to her?"

"She died a few days ago." He hands DeeDee a glass.

DeeDee takes it and drinks it immediately, "Oh my goodness, I'm sorry to hear that," DeeDee bites her fingernail.

For The Sake of Love II

While Mr. Phillips sips his drink, "Is there a problem?

DeeDee hands him the glass, "No, No, there's no problem; I'm sorry to bother you; again, my condolences." She walks toward the door.

"Your plan failed, didn't it," says Mr. Phillips

DeeDee stops but doesn't turn around, "I don't know what you're talking about."

"The hell you don't," Mr. Phillips puts his shot glass down, "you and my deceased wife cooked up this scheme to get rid of everybody that could connect Martin, your sister, and your ex-husband Chauncey." Mr. Phillips laughs, "You two didn't think I would find out, did you?"

"Again, I don't know what you're talking about."

"Okay, suit yourself, but when your sister finds out that you and my deceased wife put a hit out on her, both her sons and Chauncey, you are going to jail."

DeeDee opens the door to leave.

"That's not all; you were going to kill your mother too. That's why she was kidnapped and held up in my basement. It would have worked if your mother hadn't called me and told me what was going on. I hopped on a plane to confront my wife, and she told me everything, and I do mean everything."

DeeDee doesn't turn to face him, "So what are you going to do with this information?"

"I don't quite know yet, but if you would kill your sister, nephew, ex-husband and mother, who's to say I'm not next."

"I was protecting my family."

"You are a chip off the old block; you're just like your mother, a bitter bitch that could not handle losing a man."

"DeeDee turns to face him, "Look, old man, you got about five seconds of breath left in you. Don't make me cut it to three."

"Do what you have to do, but you should know that every person my wife hired works for me, and if anything should happen to Martin or me, the police will receive a copy of the tape. So you better hope I outlive you.

"Fuck you, fuck your tape, and fuck Martin!"

"You and your mother belong in prison."

DeeDee walks to her car, looks around, backs up, and speeds off. She starts crying and screaming.

Chapter Six
Breakdown

DeeDee has created a mess for herself; she's stolen thousands from her sister's bank account and tried to have Terri and the baby killed in a car crash, had her ex-husband killed, attempted murder on her nephew Martin and was going to have her mother killed.

DeeDee is crying, screaming, and driving all over the highway; she's losing control and barely misses hitting a car.

The police are approaching DeeDee's car with their sirens blazing, but DeeDee continues driving recklessly.

The police drive toward and behind her on the freeway to slow her down, but DeeDee decides to stop the car.

A police officer approaches her with his hand on his gun, "Ms., roll down the window and step out of the car!"

DeeDee can't stop crying.

"Ma'am, take your hands off the steering wheel and step out of the car!"

"I can't, I can't."

The officer grabs the door handle and opens the door, "Ma'am, are you okay?"

"No, I'm not okay, I want to die, please just let me die."

"Ma'am, you're not going to die, we are going to get you help."

"No, I don't want help, I want to die, please just leave me alone and let me die!"

An ambulance pulls up.

"I think she's having a nervous breakdown," says the officer.

The paramedics try to get DeeDee out of the car but she's fighting with them.

"Please, stop and just go away, I want to die."

"Ma'am we can't let you take your life, come with us and we will take care of you."

DeeDee is placed into the ambulance kicking and screaming.

The paramedics check her ID and then take her to a nearby hospital for evaluation.

DeeDee is kicking and screaming at the doctors until finally, they give her a sedative to calm her down.

For the next forty-eight hours DeeDee is heavily sedated.

Meanwhile, Chandra and Channel return from their grandparent's house and are looking for their mother.

Later that night, DeeDee still hadn't spoken, and Channel and Chandra were worried; they contacted Martin.

Martin and Otischia step in to help his sisters find their mother. After calling around to family and friends, they decide to call the hospitals.

Delores and DeeDee haven't talked in weeks.

Martin and Otishcia go back to their hotel room to chill.

Martin gets a call from his father about Mrs. Phillip's funeral arrangements, and the date of the funeral sounds familiar because it's also Terri's wedding date.

Martin looks at Otishcia, "I'm going to call Terri and ask her to postpone the wedding until after the funeral."

Otishcia looks at Martin like he lost his mind because she knows Terri and she is not going to want to postpone the day she's been waiting for not to mention the money that was paid for the wedding, "Baby you can miss the wedding, I'm sure Terri will understand.

"I want her to be here with me,"

Otishia wants him to be realistic, "It's her wedding day lots of money has been spent. Besides this is the lady that stole her baby she doesn't care about her funeral."

"She should care about me," says Martin.

"Okay, call her and let her know, you need her and see what she says."

Martin calls Terri, "Hello"

Kamal answers her phone, "Hello"

"Kamal, why are you answering my mother's phone?"

Kamal doesn't appreciate the question nor the tone, "You mean my wife's phone."

For The Sake of Love II

"Yeah whatever, let me speak to her?"

"She's busy right now with the caters, I'll tell her you called."

Martin is frustrated, "This is important, get her on the phone now."

Kamal feels like Martin is challenging him and he needs to set the record straight on who he is in Terri's life.

"Look, I'm trying to be polite to you, but man to man you need to check yourself."

"I'm not trying to hear that bullshit, get my mother on this motherfucking phone now!"

Otishcia was minding her business until she heard her man cursing, "Hey, don't do that."

Martin hangs up the phone, and he's mad.

"What is going on with you, I have never seen you like this, why are you going off on Kamal he is a nice dude and he loves your mother. Don't do this to your relationship with your stepfather."

Martin raises his voice, "I've had enough fathers in this lifetime; I don't need another one; besides, that nigga doesn't love my mother."

Otishcia stares blankly at Martin. " What," she thinks to herself, "why did you just say?"

"I just know," says Martin.

"If you know something about him, you need to let your mother know before she says, ' I do.'"

Martin's cell phone rings and it's Terri, "Hi honey what's going on is everything okay there?"

"No, it's not, my mother's funeral, I mean, well you know what I mean, is the same day as your wedding, and I really want you to be here with me."

Otishcia looks at Martin and whispers, "Don't make her choose."

Martin ignores Otishcia and waits for Terri's response.

Terri doesn't say anything right away.,

"Hello," says Martin.

"Baby, we have spent thousands of dollars for this wedding I can't just postpone it. I have over five hundred guests coming."

"Well, I won't be there, and neither will Otishcia."

Otishcia speaks up, "no, I'll be there I am a bridesmaid."

"I need you here with me." Martin insists

Otishcia and Terri are quiet.

"You know what, forget it, you go ahead and get married to that, that."

"That what, what is going on with you," now Terri is getting upset, and he is about to see another side to her, "You want me to stop my wedding for a woman who bought my child and raised him as her own and carried out a hit on my father. Fuck her, she's going to hell any motherfucking way."

Otishcia heard every word Terri said, and she knew her friend's mouth could be reckless if you pushed her.

On the other hand, Martin was shocked and speechless; he thought Terri would drop everything for him.

"What I will do is fly there and stay for a few days with you before the wedding, but I'm not postponing my wedding day for her funeral; that shit is not about to happen. I haven't been to Ohio in years, I hate that place, but for you, I will come for a day or two."

Kamal is standing nearby Terri, listening to the conversation.

Martin rubbed his hand over his head and fell back on the bed, "You're right it was wrong for me to ask you to postpone your wedding, I'm sorry."

Otishcia took a deep breath, "thank you, Jesus," she said to herself.

"I'll fly out in two days; I need to get my father situated and I'm bringing the baby with me. I'll see you then and if you need to talk I'm here."

Martin felt bad about making his mother choose, "Thank you, and again, I'm sorry."

"I love you, Martin," says Terri.

"I love you too."

Martin looks at Otishcia, I guess I was being unfair."

"You were totally being a spoiled brat, and you're too old for that, but I want to know what you know about Kamal?"

"It's nothing, seriously."

Otishcia rubs Martin's back, "Everything is going to be okay."

For The Sake of Love II

Back in Boston, "I don't think you should go," says Kamal.

Terri walks past him, "I don't want to, but I want to if that makes sense. He just lost the only mother that he has ever known, so it's natural for him to be upset. I don't want to come across as insensitive."

Kamal follows behind Terri, "Why not, he did."

Terri walks up the stairs to her closet to pack some things, "Kamal, we are not going to have this conversation, I mean, I'm going for a few days and that's that."

"So you won't ask me if you can go or if I would like to go?"

Terri drops everything and focuses on Kamal, "Did you just say ask you."

"Yes, we are a team. It's no longer you or me; it's we, and you and your son need to respect that."

Terri was not used to being spoken to like that, she was caught completely off guard, "okay, babe is it okay if I fly to Ohio to be with my son while he's grieving?"

"Sure, I think that's a great idea."

Terri chuckles, "really you wanted the right to say yes."

"No, I wanted the right to be considered, Terri. This is our marriage; you will be my wife and I have a say in every move you make and every step you take."

"Now you sound like a television commercial," says Terri.

The both of them laugh.

Kamal rubs Terri's breast and then grabs her ass, "Damn girl you are sexy as shit when you're mad."

"Hmmmmm is that so, well I can get really mad and fuck you in my closet."

"What, you're going to let Channel, Gucci, and Dior watch me bang your ass?"

Terri smiles as she places her hand on his dick, "Damn, that's what I want right there."

Kamal spins Terri around and pulls her shorts to the side and rams his dick inside of her.

"Damn, baby, I want all of it."

"I'mma give you every inch of this dick, you're my wife, and you do what the fuck I tell you to do, you got that."

"Yes, yes, yes baby, beat this pussy."

Kamal is ready to bust a nut inside Terri but she is not ready for him to cum yet, she pulls his dick out of her and turns around to face him, "Eat this pussy,"

That was not a problem for Kamal, he gets down on his knees and gets a mouth full of Terri's pussy.

Her knees buckle, "damn" she cums like the speed of lightning.

Kamal wanted his pleasure but he wanted to enter inside Terri again, "Give me another baby, he inserts himself inside Terri, and after a few minutes he lets out a chilling scream, "oh yeah, oh yeah baby."

They both are breathless but they are both satisfied.

Terri looks over at Kamal, "You really want another baby?"

"Yes I do," he's still out of breath.

"Okay but I'm going to need to take some vitamins to keep up with you."

They both laugh, and as they walk out of her closet Terri looks at Kamal's dick and it's sticky, "hold that thing, I don't want that thing touching my Gucci."

The two of them laugh as they walked out of her closet holding hands.

One week before the funeral and Terri's wedding

Terri thought about taking the baby with her but after discussing it with Kamal she changed her mind.

Terri landed in Ohio Monday morning, as soon as she stepped off of the plane she felt nauseous. Her Auntie Pam sent a car to pick her up and the two of them went to meet Martin at his hotel.

As soon as Martin saw Terri he grabbed her and hugged her, I'm so glad you came."

Terri comforts him, with a kiss on the cheek and a tight hug, "how are you doing?"

"I'm doing okay, I guess, she was my mother and I loved her."

Terri doesn't say anything.

"I know what she did was wrong but she did love me and provide for me."

"I know," Terri tries to show some feeling but deep down inside she doesn't give a fuck about Mrs. Phillips.

"I forgot to tell you about everything else that's been going on, your sister was admitted into the hospital, and from what I heard she's in the psychiatric ward."

Terri is surprised, "What, what happened to her?"

Martin explains, "My sisters said she had a nervous breakdown and the police had to take her to the hospital."

"She's right where she belongs," says Terri.

"Girl come over here and give me some love," says Otishcia

"Thank you for taking care of my son,"

"It's been my pleasure if you know what I mean."

Terri looks at Martin, Auntie Pam, and Otishcia, "so now what do we do?"

For The Sake of Love II

Back in Boston

Nina decided to drop by Terri's house, her financial report in hand, ready to share her findings and insights. It was a perfect day for a little catch-up, and Nina was eager to delve into the numbers together.

Kamal answers the door, "Hey Nina, what are you doing here?"

"Terri and I need to go over her financial reports for the quarter; if you must know."

"It's not that she and the baby left town; they went to Ohio to be with Martin. His mother died; I mean his other mother."

"I know what you mean. However, she didn't tell me."

"I thought she told you everything.," Kamal was being shady.

Nina chuckled, "I wish she did, it would help me balance her money better but I'll come back."

Martin looks down at the papers in her hand, "is there something you want me to give her?"

"No, I'll see her when she gets back."

"You know the wedding is right around the corner; can it wait until after the wedding."

"You would like that wouldn't you?"

"What is that supposed to mean? I think you should come in, and we had a talk."

"No I'll come back when my best friend is at home."

Kamal steps outside and closes the door behind him, "Nina, Is everything okay for real?"

"No, everything is not okay; there is money missing from Terri's account and excessive charges on her credit cards that don't make sense."

"Did you tell her?"

"No, that's why I'm here. Kamal, I'm just going to come straight out and ask you, did you use Terri's credit cards to pay off your debt? Because you were about to lose the Vet hospital in Roxbury, and out of nowhere, it's back up and running."

Kamal suspects Nina is questioning him: "I took out loans, and I had investors help me save my hospital. What are you insinuating, that I took Terri's money?"

"I find it strange that money was moved from her account and her credit cards right when you were about to lose everything.

"What, I didn't use her money!"

"Are you sure," Nina asked.

"Nina, you better leave because I don't want to say something that could ruin our friendship."

"I take care of your wife's finances, and if money is missing, trust me, I'm going to find it and who took it."

Nina walked to her car,

Kamal walks into the house and slams the door, and he immediately starts making phone calls.

Nina calls Terri, "Hello, why didn't you tell me you were leaving town."

"I'm sorry I forgot, I've had a lot on my plate; why, what's up?"

"I've been trying to get a hold of you for weeks to tell you your money is missing."

"What do you mean, my money is missing? I have too much money for it to be missing."

"I don't mean all of it, but someone has been writing checks, and I mean big checks from your checkbook."

"What, how much,"

"Three hundred thousand dollars altogether," says Nina.

Terri almost faints.

"Terri, what's going on?" asks Auntie Pam.

"How can we find out who it is?"

"I had the checks pulled and I looked at the signature."

Terri braces herself; she looks at Martin, "Send me a copy of the check."

"Okay, just a second; I will screenshot a check to you."

"Mom, what's wrong?"

"Someone has been writing checks from by bank account. I'm waiting for Nina to send me a copy of the check so I can look at the signature. Is there anything you want to tell me before I see the check?"

Martin is furious. "Do you really think I would steal money from you? Is that how you see me? I'm not a thief."

Otishcia walks over to Martin and Terri, "Okay, everyone, calm down."

"My money is missing I'm not calm."

"I'm being accused of stealing from you, wow. You need to look at the man you're about to marry. He's the one stealing your money."

Otishcia gasps, "oh no."

"He wouldn't steal from me," says Terri."

"And you think I would!" Martin grabs his coat to leave.

Otishcia looks at Terri, "Terri he wouldn't do that, he loves you, he really loves you."

"Well, somebody is taking my mommy goddammit."

Terri's phone rings. Nina sends the picture of the check.

Terri examines the check, after a few minutes she almost faints, "I don't believe this bitch!"

"Terri, who is it."

"It's DeeDee, she got a hold of some of your checks and cashed them." Terri's lips quiver,

Nina calls Terri, "and that's not all," says Nina.

"What, just tell me.

"Your credit cards were used to pay a loan company attached to Kamal's vet hospital."

"I'll call you when I get back," Terri hung up the phone."

"Terri, Terri, he's stealing your money!"

If looks could kill, Terri would be arrested, Terri walks out looking for Martin, "What hospital is she in?"

"What's going on," asks Martin.

Terri is noticeably upset, "I need to take care of something once and for all."

Martin calls his sisters and asks what hospital DeeDee is at; Terri, Auntie Pam, Martin, and Otishcia are on their way. Terri doesn't talk the entire ride to Mercy Medical.

Martin pulls up to the hospital.

"I'm going in by myself.," says Terri.

"No, I need to come with you," says Auntie Pam.

Terri winks her eye at her auntie, "No, I have to be alone with her."

Terri walks into the hospital, asks for DeeDee's room number, and tells the front desk she's her sister. While

Terri waits to see if she can see her, Delores, Channel and Chandra walk out and see Terri standing in the lobby.

"Terri, you came to see your sister?"

Terri slaps her mother, "No, I came to strangle her for stealing my money!" Terri grabs her mother and chokes her, "You gave her those checks, didn't you, didn't you!"

Martin saw what was happening and ran to break them apart.

"Get off of grandma, what are you doing," yells Chandra!

Terri refuses to let her mother go and Delores can barely breathe, "I hate you; I hate both of you for making my life miserable!"

Martin grabs his mother, "Mother stop!"

Terri releases her grip from around Delores's neck.

Delores wrestles to breathe.

Channel and Chandra are surprised, "your mother is our Aunt Terri," says Chandra.

"Aunt Terri, you had a child with our father," asks Channel.

Terri gathers her composure. "Yes, yes, I did, and we were in love. Your Grandmother and your mother did everything to keep him from me, and he married your mother because of her. I dated him first, and it was me he wanted, but she thought I was too ugly and fat to be with him, so she arranged for Chauncey to be with DeeDee."

"I'm confused; you had Martin. How did he get with Mr. and Mrs. Phillips," asks Channel?"

"Ask your grandmother," says Terri

Chandra turns to Delores, "Grandma, what did you do?"

Delores is speechless; she doesn't answer her.

Terri is breathing heavily, and by now, Auntie Pam and Otischia have arrived.

Terri yells at Delores, "I am going to have you put in jail along with your daughter for stealing my money, my baby, and paying to have my father killed," Terri is outraged, "I let you stay in my home, took care of you, and made sure you were comfortable and this is what you do to me, you gave her my checks, didn't you?"

Delores is crying, "Yes, because she was doing bad. Chauncey left her, and she made me do it."

"You are beneath help; you are vile, conniving, and just worthless to me; I wish you would have got an abortion instead of having me," Terri breaks down, "You never loved me!"

"I am suffering, Terri; I know I have not been the best mother to you, and I'm sorry for what I put you through, but I was hurt by your father."

"No, no, no, no, no, you don't get to use that again. You gave me life, and you did not have to make it miserable."

DeeDee hears the commotion; she walks out of her room, "what is going on out here,"

Terri lunges at her, but her son grabs her, "No, she's not worth it."

"Bitch you stole my money, you stupid bitch!"

"I'm a stupid bitch, no you need to look in the mirror because you trusted her; after everything she did, you took her in, and the rest was easy."

Auntie Pam walks over to DeeDee and smacks the shit out of her, "Don't ever disrespect my niece bitch."

Security is everywhere, Martin wants to take his mother out of the hospital so she can calm down.

"Terri points to Delores and DeeDee, "Both of you are going to rot in a prison cell when my lawyers finish with you."

They leave, and Terri's mind is racing. Her phone is ringing, and it's Kamal, but she keeps hitting "denied" on her phone. "I can't stay here; this place is evil for me."

Kamal doesn't want her to leave just yet. Before you leave, can you come with me to see my father?"

Terri is reluctant, "Sure, but I need to leave after that.

For The Sake of Love II

The next day, Terri sleeps in at her Auntie's house late, it's 12 noon and she's still sleeping. Her phone is turned off so she wouldn't be disturbed.

"Good afternoon, sleeping beauty," Auntie Pam walks into the room.

"I don't feel like sleeping beauty, I feel horrible."

"Don't let those people take you there, you are getting married in a few days, you should be on top of the world."

"I will be once those two are in prison for stealing my money, and you know what Auntie, I would have helped DeeDee if she would have asked."

"She is a product of Delores."

"Thank God I'm not."

"Your breakfast will be up shortly or lunch whichever you prefer, just relax there's no rush to get out of bed."

Terri rolls over in the bed and turns her phone on, she has fifteen missed calls from Kamal and five from Martin. Nina left her a message. "I don't want to deal with this right now."

Right before she turns the phone back off Martin calls, "Oh goodness," she answers his call, "hello," she's frustrated.

"There you are I was worried about you, are you coming with me today to see my father?"

For The Sake of Love II

Terri closes her eyes. "Yes, I'll go. Text me the address, and I'll meet you there."

"No, I want to come and pick you up; I want you to ride with me."

"Okay, pick me up in an hour," Terri says, hanging up the phone. I need to rest.

Terri decides to call Nina. "Hey, I got your message. I want to press charges against them both."

'I'm already on it. I contacted the banks and told them what happened, and you want the money back, and they said once you press charges against her, you can have all of your money back."

"Good, because that's what I'm going to do."

"What about the credit cards? What's up with that?"

"I'll handle that when I get home."

Nina hesitates but decides to ask anyway, "Will there be a wedding," asks Nina.

"Nina, I have to go now." Terri hangs up.

"I knew I should not have come here, it's nothing here for me."

Kamal is calling again; Terri denies the call again.

Terri throws the covers off of her and jumps into the shower. As the warm water hits her body, she starts to cry. Everything about her life is taking a toll on her.

Martin and Terri pulled up to Mr. Phillip's house, the sun casting a warm glow over the neighborhood. Terri, donning oversized dark sunglasses, attempted to shield her tired, puffy eyes from view. As she stepped out of the car, she paused for a moment, inhaling deeply, as if trying to gather her thoughts and muster the energy needed for the encounter ahead. The air was thick with the scent of blooming flowers, contrasting with her slightly anxious demeanor.

"Mom, are you okay?"

"Yes, son, I am fine."

Terry clung to her purse as they walked up to the door.

Mr. Phillips waited for them in the living room.

"Terri, how nice to see you; it's been years."

"Yes, sir, it has." Terri couldn't help but to hate him as well, she figured he knew all the time Martin was her baby and said nothing.

Chapter Seven
Let the Truth be Told

For The Sake of Love II

The weatherman called for a sunny, beautiful Friday, and that's just what Mrs. Phillips got on the day of her homegoing. The sun is beaming down on her horse-driven carriage as it makes it's way to the cemetery. Martin, Otishcia, and Mr. Phillips follow behind in a limousine; they console each other days before the funeral and the day of.

The time has come to lay her body to rest; a host of her friends and family members stand around holding a red rose; they were her favorite.

The Pastor gives the last words just before lowering her body to the ground, Martin breaks down into tears, he can't fight them back. He reflects on his life with his mother, the good times, they had just the two of them at the beach, in Italy and France, he remembers when she took him to Africa right before he left for college. Mrs. Phillips encouraged him to be great and always praised him, she loved him as if he were her flesh and blood.

After the funeral, family and friends gathered at the Phillip's home. Mr. Phillip had food catered. The food was impressive, and he spared no expense, and it was evident to everyone. Martin, however, was upset that there was a for sale sign on the front lawn; his mother had only been dead a few weeks, and already his father was selling their family home.

Martin, Otishcia, and Mr. Phillips are alone in the house, and Martin approaches his father about selling the house: "Dad, why are you selling our family home?"

"Son, we aren't a family anymore. Look around this big house. What do you see?"

"I see love, the love she put into this house."

"Stop being delusional, son," Mr. Phillips says, pouring himself a shot of brandy. Your mother put lies in this house; the lady was crazy."

Martin is getting mad, "Don't talk about her like that!"

"Don't raise your voice at me about her. I had to tolerate her, all while knowing it was a lie."

"You had your own lies too!"

Otishcia is starting to feel uncomfortable, "I'm going to leave and go back to the hotel."

"No, you don't have to leave," says Martin.

"Both of you need to leave. The truth is out, son. I gave you my name, my money, and my time all for her charade. You should be glad it's over. Now you and your lady friend can go and get to know your real family."

"How can you be so cruel?"

Mr. Phillips slams his glass down on the bar, "Cruel, you're calling me cruel," he walks toward Martin, "She tried to have you and your mother killed, and your father is dead because of her and Delores's daughter DeeDee. I'm not the cruel one here!"

Otishcia gasps, "What, she tried to have us killed?"

Martin looks at her, "I'll tell you about it later."

"Hell no, we're going to talk about it now; I almost died. Terri and her baby could have died, and it's because of Mrs. Phillips. She arranged to have us killed, and Terri's sister helped her, and you're standing here defending her and crying; you knew, and you weren't going to tell me; where are you? I'm leaving this house and you!"

Martin runs after her, "Wait, she told me the day she died what she had done, and she asked me to forgive her; she was sorry for what she did."

"You can forgive her, but I'm not; it's because of her I almost died; it's because of her I'll never have children."

Martin interrupts her, "Wait, you can't have kids?"

"No," Otishcia cries, "No, I can't, but what do you care?"

"Of course, I care that bullet was meant for me, not you."

"Exactly, so why are you defending her? She wanted you dead along with her secrets and lies, I can't believe you didn't tell me, Martin!"

"Please, please, Otischia, I love you, don't leave."

"I can't stand here in this house knowing what I know and Terri's own sister helped her."

Mr. Phillips tells Otishcia everything, "Yes, they were both in on it together, they wanted to keep the world from knowing the lies.

Otischia shakes her head, "this is crazy, you are crazy and I'm catching the next flight home."

"I'll take you back to the hotel and to the airport." Martin looks at Mr. Phillips, "I guess this is goodbye for us?"

"It is but not forever, I'll see you during the reading of your mother's WILL and we can keep in touch. Go and live the life your mother cheated you out of."

Mr. Phillips walks over to Martin and hugs him, "I love you, son."

Martin fights back his emotions, "I love you too."

Otischia walks back to the car dialing Terri's cell phone, but she doesn't get an answer.

Martin and Otischia are at the hotel and she immediately starts packing her clothes.

Martin sits down on the bed next to her suitcase, "can we talk?"

"You can talk, but I don't have anything to say right now."

"My mother admitted to me that she hired someone to kill me and my biological mother and father. She asked me to forgive her and then she died in my arms. I didn't have time to tell anyone what she said and the part about DeeDee helping her is all news to me, I swear I didn't know anything about that, or I would have told Terri right away."

"Bullshit, bullshit, bull motherfucking shit!" Otischia pulls up her blouse, "do you see this, do you see this scar on me, that will be on me for the rest of my life, not to mention I will never be able to have children."

Martin tries to hug her, "You didn't tell me that."

She pushes him away, "No I didn't so I guess we all have secrets."

"Otishcia, baby I love you, I was going to tell you after the funeral and the wedding."

"I don't know but all of this is too much shit for me, I didn't sign up for this Martin!" she starts to cry.

"Baby, I know, and I'm sorry I brought this into your life."

She falls into Martin's arms, "I can't have babies."

"Sit right here, I'll be right back," Martin walks over to the closet and then walks back over to her, he gets down on one knee, "I've been waiting until the right time but now is the right time, will you marry me." He opens the box and it's a six-karat diamond ring.

Otischia brings her eyes into focus, "Wow, that's a big diamond," she looks at Martin, "I can't have kids."

"I don't care, I want you."

"You say that now but you're younger than I am and one day you are going to want children; that wouldn't be fair to you."

"You almost died because of me and my crazy family, we don't know what tomorrow will bring but I know I want my tomorrow and every day after that to be with you."

Otishcia smiles, "Martin, I'm scared, I don't want to look up five years from now and some young pretty, sexy woman rings the doorbell telling me she's having your baby. I don't deserve that hurt."

"You're right and I promise you that will never happen, I give you my word, this ring, and my life."

Otishcia holds out her ring finger, "okay."

"Is that a yes?"

"Yes, yes, it's a yes, I'll marry you."

"Call your parents and let them know you said yes,"

"Wait you talked to my parents about marrying me?"

"Yep, I called them and asked for their permission; I may be younger than you but I know how to do this."

They laugh.

"Did you tell Terri?"

"She helped me pick out your ring, actually Devonna and Nina too."

"What, they all knew and didn't say anything."

For The Sake of Love II

They kiss a passionate kiss.

"I need to see my sisters before I leave," says Martin.

"I want to leave the state today; I can't stay for you to see them. I see why Terri never wanted to come back here."

"I will call them, stop by say goodbye and we can leave for the airport, I promise I won't take long."

"Their mother should be locked up in prison, not a mental hospital; she's a crazy bitch, just like Terri's mother."

Martin drifts off into a stare, thinking about what Otichia just said.

"Hello, Martin, are you listening to me?"

"Yes I was just thinking, I want to have a relationship with my sisters but I don't know how that's going to happen with their crazy mother."

"And don't forget Delores crazy ass, I feel like she started years ago."

"Yeah, you're right, all for the sake of love from my grandfather."

"You are rich you know; your biological mother is rich and your adoptive family is rich, damn."

"I'm rich because I have a woman that I love more than money."

"Oh really so you would give all the money away and just have me?"

"Would you want me if I didn't have the money?"

"Good question, but remember I dated you when I thought you were an executive at Terri's marketing firm, so the money is a plus but you had me sprung before then."

Face to face once again

Martin contacts his sisters so he can say his goodbyes but he's struggling with how to tell them about their mother's involvement with their father's murder.

Martin pulls up at his sister's house alone, it's the first time he's been to their home.

Channel opens the door, and Delores and Chaundra are seated in the living room, waiting for him to come in.

"Hi, come on in, it's nice to see you again."

"I hope you feel that way when I tell you why I'm here," says Martin.

Martin sees Delores and quickly turns to look at Chaundra, "Hello."

She rolls her eyes at Martin.

Martin is surprised at her attitude, "Excuse me have I done something wrong?"

"Yes, you knew you were Aunt Terri's son and you conveniently left that out!"

"I didn't know how to tell you, but don't be mad with me, because she knew and your mother knew too," Martin points to Delores.

Chaundra looks at Delores, "Grandma, how come no one told us our brother was also our cousin, what is going on."

"It's complicated very complicated," says Delores.

"I want to know," says Channel.

"It's not important what happened then but what is important is our father is dead because of your mother."

Delores stands up, "You're lying, Mrs. Phillips wanted you, Terri, and Chauncey dead; DeeDee was kidnapped."

"DeeDee lied about being kidnapped to throw you and everybody else off. My father told me everything. She came to the house looking for my mother and my father told her he knew everything."

Delores is speechless, "she walks into the kitchen and drinks a bottle of water."

Your mother wanted everyone connected to me dead because she is jealous of my mother; she knew Chauncey was still in love with my mother; isn't that right, Delores?"

Delores hears him, "I don't know what you're talking about!"

"Delores, please stop, stop lying, you have one foot in the grave and you're still lying and protecting DeeDee; you need to be making amends for your wrong."

Delores walks back into the living room, "Watch how you talk to me, you don't know me."

"I know you tried to have my grandfather killed, I know you ripped me from my mother and sold me to my mother and I know you didn't want Chauncey with Terri because you wanted him for DeeDee."

"You need to leave," says Delores

Channel speaks up, "No, grandmother, he will not leave, he is our brother and your grandson, I'm sick of you and my mother having secrets and controlling our lives with lies."

"He's accusing your mother of murder and you want him to be a part of your family?"

"Yep, he's our brother and if my mother did what he said, then she will have to face the consequences."

"Well, I'm not letting anything happen to my daughter."

"What about my mother, Terri, she's your daughter. Why don't you care about her?"

Delores doesn't say anything.

"Grandma, say something, she's your daughter too, Aunt Terri is a good person."

Delores hesitates, "Yes, she is, but we don't have the same relationship as your mother, and I have."

Martin shakes his head. " We don't need you," he says, looking at both his sisters. I'll be back after the wedding for the reading of my mother's will, and I'll call you."

"What about my daughter, what are you going to do with the information you now have."

"Wait and see grandma, wait and see." Martin leaves out.

/ For The Sake of Love II

Chapter Eight

A Wedding Day postponed

Terri had to postpone the wedding by one week; it cost her thousands of dollars, but it had to be done because things between her and Kamal were tense. Kamal has avoided her by working around the clock. Terri is keeping herself busy with the baby, her father, and her business, and in that order. Nina is working around the clock to get Terri's money back from the bank; however, Terri is avoiding conversations with Nina about the money that went to Kamal's business.

Terri and Kamal's wedding was mentioned in the Boston Globe and Black Enterprise magazine, and they are considered a power couple. Kamal doesn't like the attention the wedding is getting and sees this as a big problem for him, his business, and his marriage.

Four days before the wedding

It's early morning, and Terri loves to sit out on her patio and listen to the birds and take in the fresh air, it's a little chilly this morning but Terri doesn't care. The friction between her and Kamal has her head all jacked up.

Mr. Dozier's caregiver dresses him warm and then pushes his wheelchair out to the patio where Terri is.

Terri smiles as her eyes lay upon her dad's face, she doesn't care that he's old she's glad he's in her life, she knows he doesn't have much time on earth but she wants to enjoy the time they have together.

"Good morning Daddy,"

"Who are you," says Mr. Dozier.

Terri is not offended by him asking her who she is, she is well aware of Alzheimer's and his memory.

"It's me Terri, your daughter and I have your grandson here, Lil Gary."

Mr. Dozier smiles, "Hi, it's nice to meet you."

"This fresh air feels good."

"Yes it does, remember when we use to take long rides to the mountains, Delores you always loved to go to the mountains."

Terri looks at her father, "he thinks I'm my mother."

"Delores, would you like to go for a ride now."

"You want to go for a ride."

"Yes, that would be really nice."

"Okay, we are all going for a ride," says Terri.

Terri sees this as an opportunity for her and her father to have some fun and clear her head.

Terri turns on some soft music and the two of them take a ride. Terri started reminiscing about her childhood and the fun times she had with her father. It was rare because Delores didn't let him see her often but when they were together it was as if the world only had them two in it.

Mr. Dozier smiles and he talks about his past but Terri doesn't care she's happy.

Hours later:

Terri pulls back up at the house and helps her father out of the car, "Daddy that was fun."

"Yes it was Terri, you were always fun to be with, you are daddy's little girl."

Terri was surprised, "he knows it's me."

"You were the only person I truly loved in this world; I did love your mother until she tried to have me killed."

Terri sits her father down on the sofa, "Daddy you know what Delores did."

"Yes, that's why I stayed away, if she thought I was dead she wouldn't hurt you."

"You stayed away to protect me."

"Yes, I couldn't let her hurt you."

"Why didn't you come and take me from her."

"I hurt her by not standing up to my family, she should have been my wife."

Terri hangs her head, "Daddy, I wish you would have taken me from her, my life was miserable."

Mr. Dozier places his hand on Terri's hand, "Baby I'm sorry, I thought with me out of the way she would be happier."

Terri looks at her father, tears trickling down his baby's smooth skin. "It's okay, Daddy."

"Terri, can you forgive me?"

"Daddy, I forgive you."

"I saw you when you graduated from college with honors, I was so proud of you, I said, she's a chip off the old block," he laughs.

"You were there, you saw me."

"Yes, I did, I saw you from far away many times but I wanted to protect you."

"How do you forgive a woman that tries to kill you and mistreats your child?"

"My mother destroyed everything your mother loved, she took her father's cleaners, and it killed him. Your mother was strong and she lived to fight for her people. She wore her hair naturally while all the other women were getting their hair pressed. That's why I loved her, she was her own woman and unfortunately, my family didn't approve of her, she was too black for the Dozier's."

Terri can't believe his memory, but that's how Alzheimer's is, one minute you remember, and the next you don't.

Terri shakes her head, "wow I didn't know she was like that."

"Like what, where am I, who are you?"

Terri looks at her father, in a split second, he doesn't remember who she is.

"Daddy, I'm Terri, I'm going to get Grace to come and take you to your room and I'll be up later to talk to you."

"Where is Pam, I want Pam, I need to see her one last time."

Terri's eyes jump out of the socket, "One last time, what do you mean."

"I saw momma, and she told me to come home but I need to say bye to Pam first."

"I'll call her so you can talk to her."

Mr. Dozier becomes agitated, "No dammit, tell Pam to get here now, I have to go."

Terri grabs her cell phone and calls her auntie, "Auntie," her voice is trembling, my father said he needs to see you right now, something about your mother told him to say goodbye to you."

"What, I'm on my way. I was leaving tomorrow for the wedding but I can come today."

"Aunt Pam is my father is dying?"

"Terri, I'll see you when I get there."

"Noooooo, I'm not ready, please God, I'm not ready, I can't do this again."

Terri can't focus, Kamal is at work, the baby is sleeping and gifts are arriving every other second.

3 hours later

Aunt Pam is at the door, and Terri answers the door.

"Where is he?"

"He's upstairs in his room, but Auntie."

Pam walks as fast as she can up to her brother's room, "Gary it's me, it's your little sister Pammy."

Mr. Dozier tries to bring his eyes into focus, "Hi Pammy, momma told me to come home."

Pam fights back her tears, "she did, tell her I say hello."

Terri stands in the doorway.

"I love you, Pammy, take care of yourself and the family."

"I will hold it down; you can go and see momma."

"Nooooo, he can't" Terri walks into the room, "Daddy, I need you, please Daddy, don't goooo," Terri kneels by his bed.

Pam stands back and watches helplessly.

Terri calls his doctor to come and stay with him.

It's nighttime and Terri is in her bed alone again.

Terri's nerves have gotten the best of her and she can't sleep; she's tossing and turning in the bed. She throws the covers back and sits on the side of the bed, "enough is enough," she walks down to the guest room wearing nothing underneath her robe, and she opens the door; Kamal is asleep.

Terri stands at the foot of the bed staring at him while he sleeps, she calls his name, "Kamal can we talk?"

For The Sake of Love II

He hears her but fakes as if he doesn't.

"Baby, wake up, we need to talk."

Kamal decides to open his eyes, "I'm sleeping Terri, I'm on call and I need to rest."

"We need to talk about things, my father is dying and we need to talk about the money."

"Maybe we shouldn't get married."

Terri tries to play it cool, her voice trembles, "why, you don't love me?"

Kamal sits up in the bed, naked and Terri's eyes are drawn to his muscular chest.

"I love you but I realize we still have a lot to learn about each other."

Terri sits down next to him on the bed, "Like what," she knows exactly what he's talking about.

"Do you really want to have this conversation," he looks over at the clock, "at 2 in the morning."

"Everyone is expecting a wedding this week, and if we're not getting married I want to let everyone know now," says Terri.

"Okay, I was struggling in the Roxbury store, the bank was calling, and I couldn't afford to pay them. I was on the verge of losing everything, and I didn't tell you or anyone. Then, out of the sky, I get a miracle, my accountant calls me and says a donation was made to the hospital by a private organization for one hundred thousand dollars. I was happy, I was able to pay my employees and keep my three vet hospitals running; but then I got a phone call two weeks ago."

"Stop, I know,"

"Why Terri, why didn't you tell me, it was you?"

"Because I didn't think you would take the money, look, Kamal, it's a blessing and a curse being rich and most people don't know I have money. When you met me I was just a woman walking her dog, and that's how I liked it because I want a man to want me for me and not my money, but what good is having it if you can't help the people you love?"

"I didn't think you knew about my financial problems."

"I heard the phone calls, I saw the mail, what did you think I was blind and deaf."

"You had Nina thinking I took money from you."

"I didn't tell her; I didn't want her to think I was taking care of you."

"Exactly, and I don't want to be taken care of, I'm a man, Terri, and a proud one at that. I paid my way through school and I built my practice on my own. No one has ever helped me and I'm not taking money from my wife just because she's rich."

Terri lowers her head, and speaks softly, "I'm sorry, I wasn't trying to imply that you weren't a man."

"I'm going to pay you back every dime of that money, that's why I've been working all hours of the night"

Terri laughs, "why are you paying me back, I donated the money and it's a tax write-off."

Kamal stands up and his big black dick is rock hard.

"Whoa," Terri smiles.

"I have to go to the bathroom." Kamal ignores her excitement for his dick.

While Kamal is in the bathroom, Terri decides to slip off her robe and lay down.

Kamal walks back into the bedroom and his dick is still hard, "we're not done with this conversation, Terri."

Now Terri is frustrated, "What more is there to say, I was wrong for going behind your back and paying off the loan, well you were wrong for hiding it from me. We are a team, and I had to make a play without you because you were trying to keep me off the field."

Kamal starts laughing, "what are you talking about, you don't know anything about sports."

Terri laughs too, "I know but that sounded good didn't it?"

Kamal shakes his head, "this cannot happen again, we have to be straight up and honest with each other, and for the record and let everyone know, I'm not marrying you for your money. I'm marrying you for this fat ass you got girl." Kamal lays on top of Terri

For The Sake of Love II

Terri spreads her legs wide so he can slide right into her, "oohh this feels so good."

He missed Terri and it doesn't take her long to figure it out, Kamal started out passionate and then went rough on her by flipping her over on her stomach and positioning her ass up, "you want to be a team player."

Terri loves his aggressiveness and she lets him talk shit the entire time he is fucking her, her insides are exploding as she takes every inch of his dick.

There's a knock on the guest's room door.

Terri can't stop riding Kamal's dick for a second, it is too good.

The caregiver knocks again, "Ms. Terri please come it's your father."

Terri leans forward and Kamal's dick drops out of her, "My dad," Terri grabs her robe and closes it as tight as she can around her double D boobs, she opens the door, "what's wrong?"

"He's not breathing well."

"Call the doctor and 911," Terri runs to his room, "daddy, daddy."

His eyes are closed Terri doesn't know what to do.

Auntie Pam hears the commotion and she runs to her brother's room, "What's going on."

Terri gets down on her knees, "he's leaving us."

Kamal runs behind Terri after putting on some clothes. He takes his pulse and then looks at Terri and Auntie Pam.

"What, what," Terri starts crying.

Kamal hugs her, "he's dead, baby."

Terri folds in Kamal's arms, "Noooooo, noooooo."

Kamal can't fight back his tears, "he's in a better place."

"He's with momma," Auntie Pam is crying.

The next day

It's another brisk fall morning, but instead of Terri sitting on the patio playing with the baby and talking to her father, she can't get out of bed.

After the coroner removed her father's body from the house, Terri went into a deep depression. Kamal hopes the wedding will take her out of the depression.

Auntie Pam had her brother's body flown back to Ohio where he will be remembered and cremated. The day before the wedding, Terri had to fly to Ohio for her father's memorial; she was dreading going back to Ohio once again. But she had to be there.

It rained the entire day before the memorial, and it was foggy outside, so the driver of the limo could barely see. When they pulled up to the memorial, Terri was noticeably distraught. She'd been crying, but she was seated in the front row of the church in a navy-blue dress, hat, and gloves. Her dark shades hid the bags under her eyes. Kamal was seated right next to her, holding the baby, and Martin was seated on the other side of Terri.

Auntie Pam and her family are also seated in the front row of the church.

People don't know what to make of the memorial since everyone Gary Dozier knew thought he died over thirty years ago, so the attendance was very small, family only.

Terri hears crying coming from the back of the church. She turns around, but she can't make out who it is, so she turns back around again.

After the memorial, Terri walks to the back of the church and stands next to the seated woman. " How did you know? Who told you?"

The woman doesn't move or say anything.

"Who told you, dammit," Terri grabs the hat on the lady's head and pulls it off; I knew it was you; I smelled that awful perfume you wear."

Delores looks up at Terri, "I wanted to come and support you."

"You have never supported me, ever; get out; you don't deserve to be in this room!"

Everyone is surprised but Delores is really surprised.

Delores looked up at everyone and walked out of the church. "You can hate me and never speak to me

For The Sake of Love II

again, but you will never have the happiness you want until you forgive me and let go of it."

"She's right Terri, you have to let it go if you want to be happy, look at me, she lost, you won, you have the life she wanted, stop hating her," says Kamal.

Terri wipes her eyes, "I'm ready to go back to Boston and marry my prince."

The day before the wedding,

Terri decided to get a hotel suite for her entire bridal party, they are all staying at the Hyatt Regency, and Kamal and his groomsmen are staying at the same hotel but on an entirely different floor.

Kamal's friends planned to have a wild bachelor party with strippers, and lots of surprises, while Nina and Devonna are flying Terri and the rest of the bridal party to Vegas for her bachelorette party.

Terri is blindfolded as she boards the plane, "Where are you all taking me."

"Shut up, and wait," says Devonna.

Terri is anxious, she can't wait to see what's in store for her, in the meantime she's drinking and taking shots while blindfolded.

The plane lands and Devonna takes off the blindfold, "Hey bitch you're in Vegas!"

Terri looks around, okay let's get this party started and turn the fuck up!"

For The Sake of Love II

Nina is so glad Terri is excited and ready to have fun.

Back in Boston, it's ten o'clock and Kamal's party is starting to get underway, his friends have plenty of liquor and food brought into the room, and here come the women.

They make Kamal take off everything but his drawls and they blindfold him, Kamal doesn't know what's about to happen to him but just like Terri, he is game.

The music starts and Kamal's body is being touched all over, he reaches out to touch back and he feels ass, boobs, and leather.

Meanwhile, Terri is at the Hard Rock Hotel with her bridal party getting drunk and dancing with men that are getting her wet in the panties, "Oh shit, there might not be a wedding tomorrow, these men are fine as hell."

It's 1am and Kamal's party is still going strong; Kamal is the drunkest he has ever been, but he loves the asses he's watching parade around in front of him. "It's my last night as a single man, who wants this dick?"

"I do,"

"Well come and get it," says Kamal.

The woman straddles Kamal and rides him while his friends cheer him on.

Everyone is intoxicated, the other women join in on the fun.

Back in Vegas, Terri is having her share of fun as well but not the same fun Kamal is having, she's touching, feeling, and rubbing.

The ladies fly Terri back to Boston around eleven pm Vegas time. She was drunk and slept the entire flight.

Kamal's party ended around three am and he was out for the count.

For The Sake of Love II

The Wedding Day Terri has been waiting for since she could daydream is finally happening, and the only thing she won't have is her father giving her away.

Terri has been sleeping since they left but Nina, Devonna, and Otishcia haven't had time to sleep because they have to make sure Terri is put together for the wedding.

Kamal calls Terri's cell phone, "Hello," Terri is barely woke and her voice sounds like she has a hangover.

"Good morning beautiful, look out of your window.

"Kamal it's still early I'm sleepy."

"Terri, hurry up look out of your window."

Terry slowly puts her feet on the floor, "oh shit, I had too much to drink," she walks over to the window, "okay I'm here, what am I looking at."

"Wait for it," Kamal is excited.

Terri can barely keep her eyes open; she tries to stay focused, but she doesn't have a clue about what she's waiting for.

An airplane flies by her hotel room window, with a sign that says, "I LOVE TERRI DOZIER." Terri smiles, "awe, Kamal that is sweet of you."

"You are sweet and you bring out the best in me, from the day I met you walking Zoey I wanted you. We are meant for each other."

"Thank you, I didn't think love would ever find me, I dated a lot of frogs before meeting my prince." Terri is becoming emotional, "I don't want to cry now, I know I'm going to cry at the wedding."

"I am looking for to you becoming my wife, I too have had some crazy relationships and I didn't think there was anyone I could settle down with or start a family with."

"Stop you're making me cry."

"As long as they are tears of joy, that's all I care about, did you enjoy your bachelorette party?"

"Don't ask and I won't ask about yours, whatever happened last night stays a secret forever," says Terri.

Kamal laughs, "Oh okay, that's fine with me, I'll see you at 6pm."

"It's a date, handsome, wait before I forget who has the baby, I need to feed him?"

"My mother and sister have him and my mother is feeding him table food, she says it's about time."

"Oh gosh, okay, I hope he doesn't get sick."

"He'll be fine, relax and get ready for this honeymoon dick."

"You are nasty," Terri laughs, "but seriously, I'm looking forward to becoming Mrs. Bodkin."

After talking to Kamal she is woke and ready to get married, the excitement has set in, "Nina, Devonna, Otishcia, where are you!"

Nina opens her door, "look I am not the help, don't be calling me like that," Nina laughs.

Terri looks at the clock, "we don't have much time."

"Relax it's only 12, your stylist is on the way, the makeup artist is on the way, but first you need a bath, and we have someone to pamper you too."

"Great because I smell like booze, sex and I stink."

Nina fans her hand, "Yes you do."

An hour before the wedding,

Terri has been bathed, hair and makeup done, and now it's time to put on her beautiful gown, she's nervous.

Auntie Pam comes into the room, "hello gorgeous,"

"Why am I so nervous, my stomach is turning, and I feel like I can't breathe."

"All brides are nervous, you look amazing."

"Thank you I wish I felt amazing, I keep thinking about my dad not being here to walk me down the aisle."

"Well here," Pam hands her an envelope.

"What is this, I can't cry and mess up my makeup."

"Open it and find out."

Terri opens the envelope and it's a letter from her father, "he wrote this but he couldn't remember anything."

"He wrote that letter years ago, for your wedding day."

"And you kept it all these years?"

"Yes and if you had waited any longer to get married I may not have been here to give it to you," Auntie Pam laughs.

"I know, right," Terri laughs too.

"Don't read it now, read it tomorrow when you and Kamal are in Italy."

"Okay, thanks Auntie for everything you do."

"You're my baby girl too, and it's been a pleasure watching you turn into a beautiful woman."

The coordinator walks in, "Okay we need everyone out and seated so we can get ready to walk."

Nina helps Terri put her gown on "Oh my God I look beautiful."

"Yes you do, no second thoughts?"

Terri looks at Nina, "No, why would I?"

Terri hears the music playing, "It's time for me to get married."

The Wedding,

The Hyatt ballroom is filled with three hundred guests from all over the world, athletes, models, actors, actresses, and people in the music industry.

Channel and Chaundra were invited by Martin and they are star-struck.

"Who is that signing," asks Channel.

"I think that is Tank, the R&B singer," says Chaundra.

The bridesmaid walks in, each one wearing off-the-shoulder knee-length white satin dresses and holding pink flowers. The groomsmen walk in wearing white tuxedos, white bowties, and pink shirts.

Kamal walks down the aisle wearing a soft pink tuxedo, white shoes, and a white flower on his lapel.

Now it's time for the bride to walk in, Terri hears her cue to walk in and she is escorted by her son, "Are you ready mom?" Martin holds his arm out.

Terri is crying already, "I don't want to cry yet." She places her arm under his.

The ballroom doors are opened and everyone is standing up, all eyes are on Terri, and she is breathtakingly beautiful in a soft Pink fitted gown, holding a pink and white bouquet of flowers; she decided not to wear a veil, however, the train to her gown was adorned with tiny diamonds that glistened when the lights hit them. Terri went with white open-toe shoes with a two-inch heel; she was afraid of tripping and falling in higher heels.

Terri's heart is racing as she approaches Kamal she looks straight ahead at him.

Kamal's smile is big and he becomes teary watching her walk toward him.

Finally, she is at the altar and Martin releases her arm, kisses her on the cheek, and whispers in her ear, "I love you."

Terri stands in front of Kamal; she looks over at their son sitting on his grandmother's lap and then waits for the Minister to speak.

Everyone takes their seat; Martin is seated next to his two sisters.

"If anyone feels these two should not be joined, please speak now or forever hold your peace."

"They should not be married," yells one of the guests!"

The other guest gasped; Terri looks to see who said something but the camera's lights are flashing in her eyes.

The woman tried to make her way toward the front, but security stops her, "she fucked my husband," says Renee.

"Oh, my God," says one guest.

"And my daughter fucked him, Kamal had sex with my daughter Tracie and she is pregnant," yells Renee.

Terri looks at Kamal and then runs out of the ballroom.

Martin, Nina, and Auntie Pam run behind her.

Chapter Nine

For The Sake of Love II

What just happened to Terri's big day?

Terri runs out of the ballroom, holding her beautiful bouquet in one hand and her gown in the other.

Kamal is speechless; his groomsman steps up to him, "What is going on?"

Kamal looks at his mother, "I'm sorry," he whispers.

"Go after her, go and get your wife," says Kamal's mother.

Kamal walks and then runs out of the ballroom looking for Terri, "Terri, Terri," he's looking everywhere.

He sees Nina, "where is she?"

"How could you do this to her, why would you do this to her, she loves you, Kamal?"

"Nina, just tell me where she is!"

"No, she left and she said she said she doesn't want to see you."

Kamal is pacing the floor, "What about the baby, she's not going to leave our son."

"Martin will bring him to her, but she doesn't want to see you."

"Nina, please, I love Terri, this didn't just happen, why am I explaining to you? I need to talk to Terri."

Nina shakes her head, I thought you were the one for her."

'I am, Nina, please don't let the guests leave, just tell me where she is and let me make this right."

"She went to her hotel suite."

Kamal takes the elevator to the eleventh floor and runs off. He is sweating profusely. He stops at her room and hears her crying, "Terri, baby, let me come in so we can talk."

"No, get away from me; how could you, Kamal, go away."

Meanwhile, Nina is explaining to the guest and the coordinator that everything is okay.

"I knew it was going to come out sooner or later," says Martin.

"You knew he cheated on your mother and you didn't say anything?" Otischia is livid.

"I wasn't sure, but I suspected he was or did."

"Martin, I don't believe you, why would you sit on something like this?"

"I didn't want to hurt her, and I wasn't sure she would have believed me. We are building our bond and I didn't want to mess it up by telling her, her fiancé was cheating with Renee's daughter."

"Oh so you did know it was her, you just lied to me."

"Tish this is not our argument, I need to check on my mother."

"No," she pulls him back, "this is a job for her best friends, she needs us right now."

Kamal is standing outside her hotel room door trying to explain, "Terri, Tracie came in with her dog and she flirted with me, and it was around the time when I was losing my mind, my business and I thought you too. I had sex with her a few times but I didn't know she was Renee's daughter, I swear."

"Unprotected sex, you went into that bitch raw!"

Kamal hesitates, "yes."

"Did you know she was pregnant before today?"

"No, I swear to you I didn't know, I haven't seen or talked to her; I told her months ago it was over and I couldn't see her anymore."

"You couldn't see her or you didn't want to see her?"

"Terri," Kamal gets down on one knee in his white tuxedo, "my exact words were, I love my fiancé, and I don't want to see you anymore."

"You love me, but that didn't stop you from fucking her or being with her, did you feel anything for her?"

"It was me being stupid and not accepting my financial problems."

Terri walks over to the door and opens it, she slaps Kamal across his face, "You are a big dummy, Renee played you and me."

"What are you talking about?'

For The Sake of Love II

"I fucked her husband, and I thought our baby was his; this bitch goes missing, and then her daughter shows up at your vet hospital with a dog and flirts with you. They set your weak ass up and you fell for it."

"So what are you saying?"

Nina, Otishcia, and Devonna are down the hall listening along with other guests at the hotel.

"Renee would do anything to get back at me, the bitch went missing and had everyone looking for her and now she shows up trying to destroy my wedding." Terri grabs her bouquet, "let's go."

"Where are we going to?"

"We're getting married, that bitch is not stopping my wedding," she looks at Kamal as they walk toward the elevator, "that was your one and only pass." They walk past Nina, Otishcia, and Devonna in the hallway. "let's go, I'm getting married, fuck that bitch I'll deal with her ass later."

Terri looks like she's ready for a war.

They all ride down the elevator together,.

"Terri are you sure you want to marry this man, he did cheat on you," says Devonna.

"Devonna, shut the hell up and mind the business that pays you," says Nina.

"Yes, I'm getting married and not because I'm desperate for a husband, but because I'm not perfect and I've fucked up. This man stayed with me after I told him I didn't know if he was the father of our child or not. He could have left but he stayed and for that, I can forgive him for his foolish dick escapades."

They step off the elevator and Kamal walks back down to the front and stands.

Terri sees Martin, "walk me back down."

"Mom, no, he cheated on you."

"I know, but I've done some things that I'm not too proud of either and he forgave me, besides, I'm not letting Renee have the last laugh. I took her husband and made him eat out of my hands and some other places that I can't tell you and that bitch is mad. I'm not letting her madness ruin my life."

Martin looks at her concerned she's making a big mistake, "Okay but I hope you know what you're doing?"

Terri winks her eye at him, "I do, now walk me down the aisle so I can marry my man."

The coordinator is about to lose her mind; her glasses are falling off of her face, and her hair is frizzy. "I'm going to have to add on to my fee because I wasn't expecting all of this,"

Terri looks at her and smiles, "Calm down, I'll take care of you."

The coordinator cuts the music, and the door to the ballroom is opened once again, and everyone is

For The Sake of Love II

standing again. Terri tries to focus on Kamal, but whispers from the guests are taking her focus away.

"Are you okay," asks Martin.

"I'm fine, I'm not going to allow what they think to ruin my big day."

Meanwhile, Renee is outside of the Hyatt causing a disturbance.

Terri has prepared her vows for Kamal,

"I thought finding love was a myth or it only happened for the really pretty girls, but then a thoughtful, loving man walked into my life and changed my mind." Terri can hear the whispers, but she continues and ignores them, *"Kamal I want to thank you for your love, kindness, and most of all our son. I will respect you, love you and stand beside you in the good and bad times."*

Kamal pulls out his vows, he's nervous and his hands are shaking.

He has everyone's undivided attention; it is dead silent in the ballroom.

Kamal looks at Terri, looks at what he wrote, and then folds the paper up and puts it back in his jacket. He reaches out for her hand, *"Terri, I am human, I have flaws, I am not perfect and I'm asking you to be my wife knowing that I will never be perfect. What happened in my past will never happen again, I will not keep secrets from you, and I will be one hundred percent transparent to you."* He pulls out his paper *again, "My love, you are beautiful inside and out, you inspire me to be the best version of myself and I want to be the man that you can count on, lean on and grow older with. I accept you for who you are, the good the great, and the better version of you. I want to stand with you, not in front of you or behind you, even though it's a great view back there."*

Everyone laughs, including Terri.

"She paid for that nice view," Devonna whispers to Otischia.

Otischia rolls her eyes, "Devonna, please make an appointment for a new ass, your jealousy is annoying," she whispers back.

After the vows, Kamal places the ring on Terri's finger and you can see the diamond from the back of the ballroom. Terri had Kamal's ring custom made with ten karats of diamonds. The Minister pronounces them husband and wife and Kamal steps toward Terri and throws her back and kisses her passionately.

"Wow, that was a kiss," says Terri.

"There's more where that came from.

Kamal's mother hands them the baby and the three of them walk out of the ballroom, holding hands.

Terri goes back to her hotel room to change along with Kamal while the guests are seated for the reception.

Kamal looks at Terri, while her assistant helps her out of her dress, "how do you feel."

"What do you mean?"

"We're married now, don't you feel something."

"Honestly, I feel like Renee needs her ass whipped along with her daughter but as far as you and I, I feel like Karma bit me in the ass."

"Why do you say that?"

"How did you feel when I said I don't know who the father is and you had to take a DNA and you found out I was sleeping with Rob."

"I was devastated but I needed to put that aside because you were sick."

"Exactly, you felt comfortable fucking someone else because, in the back of your mind, she did it."

"So, what are you a shrink now?"

"Kamal, it doesn't take a doctor to see what happened."

"Are we going to survive this, tell me now because I don't want a divorce?"

Terri kisses his lips, his face all over, "If I wasn't okay, trust me, we would not be wearing these rings."

Kamal smiles, "Okay, let's change and go downstairs and party!" He's excited

Terri changes into a short, deep V-neck all-white short body-com dress, while Kamal changes into an all-white suit.

They show up at the reception, have their first dance, and enjoy their guest. Devonna and Otishcia are starstruck, they didn't know Terri knew any of these people.

Meanwhile, Renee and her daughter Tracie are not far, they parked just outside of the hotel and positioned themselves to see when Terri and Kamal leave the venue.

Renee is laughing, "You should have seen her face when I said you were pregnant, I finally got that bitch back."

"Mom, do you think they still got married?"

"Yes, I think they did," Renee is watching the door through binoculars.

"Mom, please why are you so obsessed with her, it's too much, they're married now."

"But you are carrying his child, that means if he married her you get some of that money and we are rich."

"Oh, shit I didn't think of that."

"Leave it to your mother to think of everything, I planned all of this and it's going to work, trust me. She is going to regret ever fucking your father."

"Have you talked to dad lately?"

"I'm avoiding him because he wants a divorce."

"Mom the man had an affair and he fell in love with her, let him go."

Renee is getting choked up with emotion, "I love your father, and I know if it wasn't for her he and I would still be together."

Five hours later and the reception is still going on, Brian McKnight sang, CeCe Piniston sang, and DC Young Fly, it is a wedding reception Terri's friends and family won't forget.

It's ten o'clock at night, Tracie is tired of waiting around and she's ready to go home, "Mom, please can we leave, I'm tired and I need to lay down."

Renee doesn't want to leave yet, "call him, call his cell phone and see if he answers."

"He's not going to answer, he blocked me when he told me he didn't want to see me anymore."

"Call from my phone dammit, look I need you on board with this."

Tracie sighs, "hand me your phone, she calls Kamal from Renee's phone.

Kamal's phone is upstairs in his hotel room.

"He's not answering mom, now let's go, I really need to lay down," Tracie is upset.

"Alright, alright but I need to find a way into that hotel before they leave for the honeymoon."

"Take me home and you can do whatever you like," says Tracie.

"I'm doing this for us, do you know the money we can get?"

"First you go missing so she can get arrested, and that didn't work, and now I'm pregnant with no man, and how is that working for us, I shouldn't have let you talk me into this."

"When we are vacationing on yachts and living with the rich and famous I want you to remember this."

Renee drives off to take Tracie home but she is planning to drive back.

Terri and Kamal have a private flight to catch at two in the morning, so they decided to take the baby, nanny, and champ and Zoey with them on the honeymoon.

For The Sake of Love II

Terri and Kamal wake up together in a beautiful villa in Venice Italy.

Terri walks onto the patio and looks up at the sky; its beautiful clear sky captivates her mood, "I see you got out of bed before me." She kisses Kamal on his cheek.

He takes her by her waist and places her on his lap, "Good morning Mrs. Bodkins,

Terri likes the sound of her new name, she smiles, "I like that.

"You do, you really don't mind changing your famous name to my plain name?"

Terri chuckles, "I'll always be Terri worth millions, that will never change."

Kamal hears his phone ring.

"Get the phone it might be the hospital."

"No, I'm not on call and they know I'm in Italy with my family."

Kamal looks at his phone, "I don't recognize this number anyway."

Terri opens up the paper and there it is, her wedding and pictures of Renee and the debacle that happened at the wedding "Oh my God, this is a hot mess, I better get my publicist on this."

Kamal doesn't want to deal with any of that stuff, "Nope, you and I are going to enjoy this week we have together, we can deal with that when we get back."

For The Sake of Love II

Kamal, Terri, and their son enjoy the scenery of Venice, Terri shops while Kamal and the baby tag along. The family spent hours and hours making love and talking about their future, it was as if the world outside of their villa didn't exist.

The week was quickly ending and Terri is not ready to leave yet she wants to stay another week, but her husband has a practice he needs to attend to.

Kamal left to walk Champ and Zoey while Terri lays in the bed, Kamal's phone rang and she decides to answer it, "Hello,"

"It's her, it's her, "says Tracie.

Renee takes the phone, "Hello,"

Terri recognized her voice immediately, "yes Renee, what does your daughter want."

"Ah yeah, bitch you recognize my voice."

"Of course, your cigarette raspy voice, I would recognize it anywhere."

"Whatever, I made the front paper for crashing your wedding."

"Yes, and you could have at least worn pink so you could blend in with the rest of the elite, I honestly don't know how you got in, but I'll take that up with security, anyway how can I help you?"

"Well since your husband has a baby on the way with Rob and my daughter, I need to speak to him about support."

"I honestly thought you were dead," Terri laughs, "you pimped your daughter to fuck my husband and now you're calling to extort money from him."

Renee wasn't ready for Terri's venom, "Bitch I didn't pimp my daughter."

"Sure you did, she walks into the vet hospital with a dog I assume is really hers this time, and flirts with my sexy ass husband, he fucks her and now she's pregnant. Yeah bitch, you pimped her."

"Your husband was weak for pussy."

Terri sits up in the bed, places her feet on the floor, grabs her robe, and walks over to the bar, "like her daddy." Terri pours a glass of 1800 vodka.

"You seduced my husband with your implants, he told me your ass was like rubber."

"And he bounced all of it with his face, now I'm not going to get too many phone calls from you to my husband's phone or you will be missing for real this time."

"Is that a threat?"

"How many months is your daughter anyway?"

"She's five months pregnant," says Renee.

"Oh good, a January baby, I hope it's a girl so our son can have a sister."

"Bitch you will never touch my grandchild."

Terri finishes her drink, "that's the last bitch for today, we will order a DNA, and then if it is my husband's baby we will raise him or her because let's be clear; I have enough influence in Boston to make your daughter unfit. Renee, do not fuck with me or my family or I am going to."

"Do what," says Renee

"Well watch me, you seem to like to do that, and by the way, where's Rob, are you to still together?"

Renee hangs up.

"Exactly what I thought."

Terri pours herself another drink.

Kamal is back with the dogs, he kisses Terri, "whoa you have been drinking."

"I had a few, hell I'm on vacation and your phone rung, it was Renee and Tracie."

"What did they want?"

"To piss me off."

"Did it work," Kamal chuckles?

"Hell no, I'm in Italy,and on my honeymoon with my family, Nothing and I do mean nothing could possibly piss me off." Terri pours herself another drink.

"Take it easy, honey."

"I just got started, oh and before I forget I'm not ready to leave, let's stay another week."

"I have to see if I can get another doctor to cover the hospitals, I'll call and see."

"I'm not ready, and I'm flying Martin and my nieces out here."

"You are, when were you going to tell me, Terri that's a lot of money." Kamal is concerned.

"Okay, I'm paying for it."

"That's not the point, Terri and you know that."

"Your mother and sister can come too."

"No, they cannot, I'm not in a position to fly them out here and put them in a villa for a week, do you know how much that costs?"

Terri is at the bar pouring herself another drink, "no I don't but I'm sure I have enough in my account to cover it."

Kamal walks over to the bar and takes the glass out of her hand, no more it's not even 12 o'clock in the afternoon.

"It's 12 o'clock some motherfucking where," she takes the glass back from him and drinks the vodka.

"Terri, please stop drinking."

Terri grabs her sunglasses, "Babe, loosen up and enjoy your family, me, and our son."

Kamal pours himself a glass of brandy."

"Yes, thank you, relax," says Terri.

Kamal was able to get a doctor to cover for him and they stayed another week with his family and hers.

The Honeymoon is over.

Terri and Kamal are back from the honeymoon and two months later people are still talking about Renee's attempt to ruin the wedding.

Terri is back at the helm of Dozier Marketing with Martin as her Chief Operating Officer, and Martin is making his mother very proud.

Kamal is back to work doing what he loves, saving and delivering animals.

Even though Terri is back to work she can't stop thinking about her dad dying, her mother betraying her, DeeDee stealing from her, and Renee's daughter being pregnant by her husband; all of that has Terri pouring vodka, one drink after another.

The ladies haven't had a girl's night out since Terri's bachelorette party; Nina planned a night out for the four of them in her hometown of Baltimore, Maryland at the MGM. Terri can't wait to get away.

They check into the MGM and Terri heads straight to the bar, and all eyes are on her.

"Are you drinking heavily again," asks Devonna.

Terri is not for Devonna's bullshit, "I'm not sharing a room with her am I?"

"Actually we all have separate rooms, I'm not making that mistake again," says Nina.

"Good, because I do not want to be monitored I left my husband at home."

"Well, mother-in-law, Martin and I have set a date to get married."

"When is that," Terri's speech is a little slurred now.

"I want a winter wedding; we're getting married in February."

"Are you crazy February, it's cold as hell and it may not happen because of the snow."

"The wedding will be in Dubai," says Otischia.

"His momma can afford it, she's a rich bitch," says Devonna.

"And don't you forget it," says Terri.

"My parents are paying for my wedding, thank you very much."

"I'm going to hit the slot machines and I'll catch up with yawl later," says Terri.

Nina walks up to Terri, "you have had too much to drink, you need to chill the fuck out, seriously."

Nina rarely said anything to Terri so when she spoke Terri listened.

"Okay, I'll go up to my room and sleep it off, okay mother."

"I'm not your damn mother," Nina laughs.

Terri catches the elevator up to her room.

The elevator door opens and a man walks onto the elevator; Terri doesn't make eye contact right away but the man notices Terri.

"Excuse me,"

Terri looks up, "Oh my God."

"Hey what are you doing here?"

"I'm, "Terri thinks should she lie, "with my girlfriends."

"It's nice seeing you," says Rob.

Terri's floor is next, "You too,, she steps off of the elevator, "what is he doing here?"

Terri hurries into her room and locks the door, "this is more than a coincidence, I'm sure."

All of the other ladies are gambling and having fun while Terri is resting.

Three hours later Terri is up, sober, and ready to hit the slots, she calls Nina, "Nina where are you, I'm feeling better I'm at the casino."

"I'm in my room resting we are tired, go and do you, be careful, we're close to Baltimore, these fools are crazy."

"I'm good," instead of playing slots Terri decides to play the tables, she takes a seat and asks for one thousand dollars in chips and she starts betting. When she wins she gets excited and when she loses she curses. The waitress handed her five drinks in the last two hours.

Rob passes by and hears Terri's voice, he walks over in her direction, and there's a seat next to her. He takes a seat right next to her.

Terri looks over and sees him and smiles, "hello again."

"Hello again to you," says Rob.

Terri felt a little weird but she continued gambling, and the more she gambled the more she drank. The clock is moving, it's four in the morning and Terri has had enough.

Terri walks away from the table with five thousand dollars worth of chips.

Security walks over to her, Mrs. Terri, do you need an escort to your room for your safety"

"No, no, I'm a little tipsy but I can make it to my room, I'm okay, how do you know my name anyway?"

"You are very well-known ma'am and we make it our business to know who's who."

Terri walks to the elevator alone and when she steps on, Rob steps on behind her, she turns around, "You scared me, what are you following me."

"I guess you could say that."

Terri is getting crazy vibes from him, "What do you want, Rob?"

"I want you, bitch," he punches her and Terri is out cold in the elevator.

Rob takes the elevator up to his room along with Terri, he picks her up and carries her in his arms.

The next morning,

The ladies meet for breakfast, Devonna, Otishcia, and Nina are waiting on Terri before they order.

"Where in the hell is Terri," asks Otischia?

"Probably upstairs passed out drunk, again," says Devonna.

"Devonna, please not now, I got a weird feeling something is wrong, I'm going up to her room," says Nina.

Nina, Otischia, and Devonna leave and go to Terri's room and knock on the door; after knocking and no answer Nina calls the hotel lobby and asks to get in.

Room service opens the door and Terri is not there, but her luggage is.

"Somethings wrong, oh no, where is Terri," says Nina!

Chapter Ten
Snapped

For The Sake of Love II

It's been twenty-four hours and Nina, Devonna and Otischia haven't seen or heard from Terri and they are not able to trace her whereabouts on her cell phone.

Devonna believes she will show up and they need to stop worrying but Nina has a strange feeling something is wrong.

While Terri's friends are frantically looking for her, Rob knows exactly where she is, that's because he has Terri tied up by her legs and hands and has a gag over her mouth in his hotel room.

Nina is falling apart and that's rare for her because she's the one that always has it together, "I'm scared something bad has happened to Terri," she looks at her watch, "our flight leaves in two hours and we can't leave without her."

Devonna is not in agreement with the other two ladies, "I'm leaving without her; I have a husband to get home to. I can't stay around here looking for a drunk who obviously strayed off to do what she wants to do. That's how she is you know, she does whatever she wants to and Nina you cater to her. You need to stop catering to Terri and marry Vince, Terry has her husband what about you?"

"Devonna, stop!"

Nina startled both of them.

"Oh, snap I didn't know the girl could holler," says Otischia

"Shut the fuck up, I am sick and tired of your mouth Devonna, Terri has been nothing but nice to you, all of us as a matter of fact, and I don't cater to her. I happen to know what real friendship is unlike your fake ass. The reason I'm not married to Vince, is because I'm not ready to get married, it's my life and my decision. I've been a wife and I didn't like it much so I'm not ready to take that walk down the aisle, again."

"Well excuse me," says Devonna.

Nina is mad, "You're not excused, as a matter of fact, let me call you a cab and you can see your way to BWI airport and catch a flight back to Boston to be with your husband."

"Nina, calm down."

"Bitch, I am calm."

Devonna doesn't like that, "Wait a minute, you're not going to call me names and think I'm supposed to take it."

"I called you a Bitch, now what," Nina steps toward Devonna.

Otishcia steps in, "Wait, wait, wait, we need to refocus and find Terri," Otischia stands between them. "Devonna, catch a flight out to be with your husband and we'll stay here and find Terri."

"You kiss her ass because she's rich," says Devonna.

"I've never asked Terri for anything, nothing, money, houses, cars absolutely nothing and she has offered me houses, cars, clothes, purses, trips, and I always say no. She's like family to me and I work for her so I earn my money."

"She's telling the truth, "Says Otischia.

"She's never offered me anything," says Devonna.

"She ain't stupid, she knows her friends from her enemies," says Nina.

"Okay ladies, enough, Devonna if you're leaving, leave and if you're staying, shut the fuck up and let's find Terri."

Nina walks away from Devonna to call the police.

Otischia wants to find Terri, she doesn't have time for the mess, "What are you going to do Devonna?"

"Tish I have to go home to my family and I have to go back to work, I don't have money like Terri."

"Fine, there's the door," says Otischia.

"I'll be praying for Terri, but I really think, she's just drunk in some man's room."

Otischia laughs, you really don't know Terri do you, she would never do anything like that, she has a child and a husband not to mention she's not freaky like that. Just say it, you don't like her, deep down inside you don't like her."

"I like her, I'm just not going to kiss her big ass."

'You see, there you go again, you're jealous of her, girl bye."

Devonna walks over to Nina and taps her on the shoulder, "I'm leaving, can I get a hug, we're sisters too.

Nina ignores her and continues talking to the police.

Devonna and Otishcia hug, "you're our stepsister," Otishcia laughs.

"Funny, not funny," Devonna leaves and goes to her room to pack, she starts thinking about her friendships with all of the ladies, "I'm not jealous of Terri, I just think she thinks she's better than us and I'm not kissing her ass."

Devonna is packed, she booked her flight, called her husband, told him what was going on, and called an uber to take her to the airport.

Devonna steps onto the elevator, there's a man on the elevator wearing black jeans, a black hoodie, and black sunshades. Devonna looks at him, and smiles, "Good morning."

He doesn't answer her,

Devonna looks at the man again, "Hmm he looks familiar, that's the guy Rob that was obsessed with Terri, his wife tried to ruin her wedding," she says to herself.

The elevator doors open on the main floor and Devonna steps off first and then Rob.

For The Sake of Love II

"Excuse me, sir."

Rob turns to Devonna.

"You're Rob, Terri's old friend, and neighbor, right?"

Rob walks off without answering her.

"I know that nigga, that's Rob." Devonna pulls out her cell phone to call Nina and Otischia.

Rob walks up from behind Devonna and places a gun on her side, "Put the phone away and don't say anything, just walk."

Devonna is startled, she turns around, "What, oh my God,"

"Walk, and don't make any moves." Rob snatches her cell phone and throws it in the trash can.

"Wait, I don't know who you are" Devonna is trembling.

Rob grabs a hold of her hand," "Walk and shut up," he walks her back into the MGM and they take the elevator up to his room without looking suspicious.

Rob opens the door and shoves Devonna in the room, "That's what you get for opening your big mouth."

Devonna sees Terri tied up, "Oh my god, Terri," she looks over at Rob as he walks toward her, "wait, I have nothing to do with her, this, or anything. Please let me go and I won't say anything."

Terri tries to scream but her mouth is tied up, tears streaming from her eyes.

Rob grabs a chair and throws Devonna in the chair and starts tying her up by her legs and hands.

"Wait, wait, please let me go, my husband will be looking for me," Devonna is pleading for her life.

"Shut up, lady, you see what you made me do Terri, now I have to kill both of you!"

Devonna is terrified, and she starts crying.

Meanwhile, Nina and Otischia think Devonna is on her way home, they have no idea she's just a few floors above them and being held captive along with Terri.

The police arrive at the hotel and they start checking through the security cameras for a trace of Terri.

Nina receives a call from Kamal, "oh no, it's Kamal, should I tell him what's going on?"

"Yes, tell him because we don't know what's going on and we need him, I'm going to call Martin and let him know."

"Hello,

"Hey Nina, where's Terri, I've been calling her and she's not answering; the phone is going straight to voicemail."

Nina looks at Otischia, and then takes a deep breath, "Kamal I have some bad news."

"What, what, what happened to Terri?"

"We haven't seen her in twenty-four hours, she was gambling early Friday morning, and Saturday we went to her room and she wasn't there."

"DAMMIT NINA, WHY DIDN'T SOMEONE CALL ME!"

"We didn't want to worry you for nothing, we called the police, and the hotel security is working with us to find her."

"I'm on my way there."

"Kamal, wait,"

Kamal hung up, left work, called the house assistant, and had her put some clothes in a bag and schedule his flight for Maryland.

Meanwhile, Rob is pacing the floor, he did not plan on killing two people."

He looks at Devonna, "Now I have to kill you too."

Rob kneels down in front of Terri, and he unties her mouth.

Terri pleads with him, "Rob, please let her go, don't do this, I'll give you whatever you want, just let Devonna go."

"No, no, no, shut up, and let me think."

Terri tries to play nice, "what do you want baby?"

"I wanted you, I wanted to marry you and have a baby with you. I wanted you to be all mine," Rob kisses her lips.

"We can still do that, I'll divorce Kamal, I don't love him anyway, I only married him because he was the baby's father. It's you I really love." Terri is lying but she needs him to believe her.

"Really, you love me?'

"Yes, the way you make love to me, and hold me, no one can replace that."

Rob smiles, "you're lying!"

Terri lowers her voice to seduce him, "Baby don't you remember how I use to lick the cum off your dick."

Rob's dick jumps, he is instantly hard.

Devonna is praying for Terri's plan to work.

"Baby it's you I wanted, I swear, you know I love you."

"Why did you marry him, Terri, I would have taken care of you and the baby?"

"I'll divorce him, I can have it annulled and you and I can get married."

"He took you from me, I wanted to kill him, but you, you let it happen."

"I was wrong, he cheated on me with your daughter and now they are having a baby, and you and I can be together."

"That's not his baby, Renee planned that bullshit, that's Tracie's boyfriend's baby."

Terri can't react to what he just said, she has to keep him at the moment, "I don't care, it can be me and you, baby."

Rob is getting weak, "Really, really Terri," he hugs her, "I love you so much."

"Untie me, so we can be together, we can go into the other room and make love like we use to."

Rob is happy, "what about her, what are we going to do with her," he looks at Devonna.

"You can let her go; you don't want to kill her."

"I have to kill her, her husband and I work together, he is the one that told me where you would be this weekend. He said his wife and her friends were going to the MGM for a weekend girls' trip."

"You know Devonna's husband?"

"Yes, I know him and Nina's boyfriend too."

"How do you know Vince," asked Terri.

"I made it my business to know everyone close to you," Rob stands up, and starts pacing again, "Can I trust you, or you?" He's waving the gun.

Terri looks over at Devonna she doesn't know what to say.

"Rob, baby, I haven't had great sex since you, you look good, baby take me to the room and fuck me."

Rob walks over to untie Terri, "If this is a trick I am going to blow your brains out and then I'm going to kill her. I don't have anything to lose."

"No, no this is not a trick, I want you inside me."

Rob unties Terri's legs but not her hands, "No sudden moves or you're dead."

Terri has never seen anyone up close and personally look so sinister, she's scared to death.

He leads her into the other room and throws her on the bed, he starts taking off her clothes.

"Baby, untie me, I want to enjoy you."

"Wait," Rob takes his clothes off, and he begins to have sex with Terri.

Her hands are still tied behind her back, but she pretends to enjoy it, but her flesh is crawling with disdain for Rob.

"Untie so I can join in."

"No, I'm in control," Rob refuses to untie her.

"Okay, baby," Terri doesn't want to get him angry.

Devonna is in the other room listening and crying, she tries to loosen up the straps on her feet and hands.

Rob is fucking Terri like a madman and typically she would be enjoying it but not this time, she has no feeling at all.

Rob is starting to feel Terri is not enjoying him, he stops, "You don't want me?"

For The Sake of Love II

"Baby, you have me tied up, I feel like a prisoner, I feel like I'm being raped."

Two hours later, Nina, Otishcia, and the police are watching hotel footage.

Otishcia called Martin to tell him about his mother and he called Kamal and now the two of them are on their way to Maryland.

Nina and security are watching the cameras and they see Terri walking on the elevator and then they see her being carried by a man with a hoodie on.

"What room is he taking her into?"

"That's the ninth floor and room 910," they check the name that room is registered to," It's Registered to Robert C,"

Nina puts it together, "oh my God, that's Robert, that's Terri's old neighbor, Renee's husband. He was stalking Terri because she dumped him, but how would he know we would be here."

Two hours later, Kamal and Martin's private plane land in Maryland, and there's a ride waiting for them.

Kamal calls Nina, "hey have you heard anything from Terri, what's going on."

"The security cameras see her being carried to a room and they are on their way to the room."

"Drive faster," Kamal yells at the driver

"The room is registered to Robert C."

"The man that she use to fuck with!"

"Yes," says Nina.

"Hurry up, and get me to the MGM, I'm going to kill that nigga."

Martin is mad, "I told him if he ever came anywhere near her I would kill him"

Kamal pulls a gun out of his duffle bag, "Naw, I got his ass, he fucked with the wrong wife."

Hotel security and the police get off the elevator and walk quietly to room 910, they knock on the door, "Housekeeping,"

Devonna wants to scream but she can't, she fights to untie herself.

Rob and Terri can't hear the knocking.

Devonna can get one hand out, and she uses it to untie herself, she's out of breath, "Oh thank you, Jesus, she walks over to the door and opens it, "help, help us."

"Shhh, where is he,"

"He has her in the back room, he's raping her, he's going to kill her," Devonna is hysterical

The hotel security take Devonna out of the room,

Martin and Kamal pull up at the hotel and take the elevator up to the 9th floor.

The police ease into the room, and they can see Rob on top of Terri.

Terri spots the police, "baby let me get on top, please I want to ride your dick."

Rob has forgotten all about he is holding her captive, he flips Terri over on him.

Terri jumps off of Rob.

The police rush into the room, "Don't move!"

Terri is crying, "I hate you; I hate you; I hope you die!"

The police handcuff Rob and walk him out of the hotel room.

Kamal and Martin get off of the elevator and Kamal pulls his gun out to shoot,

The police pull their weapons.

Martin pulls his weapon and fires and hits Rob.

The police fire their weapons and hit Martin and Kamal several times.

Terri hears gunshots and she runs out of the room with a sheet wrapped around her; she sees Martin and Kamal on the ground, "Noooo, nooo, it's my husband and my son, call 911!"

The police call 911 for Rob, Martin, and Kamal.

Nina and Otischia still don't know that Devonna is up on the 9th floor and was held hostage with Terri.

Martin was shot in the stomach, Kamal was shot in the neck and Rob was shot in the chest, all three have life-threatening gun wounds.

Terri is hysterical, please don't let my son and husband die, save them.

Three ambulances pull up, to take care of Kamal, Martin, and Rob.

Nina and Otishcia finally get to see Terri, and they run to her; Terri is crying, "he was going to kill us."

"Who is us, was there someone else in the room with you," asks Nina.

"Yes, Devonna he was holding me and Devonna!"

"Calm down, no, Devonna left this morning, she caught a flight out of BWI."

Terri tries to explain, "No, no, she recognized him on the elevator so he grabbed her and put a gun to her and made her come back to the room."

"Oh no, where is she now!"

"I don't know, she ran out as soon as the police came in."

Terri tells Otischia about Martin, "Tish, the police shot Martin, please go check on him."

Devonna is downstairs in the lobby talking to the police and telling them what happened.

Nina goes down to the lobby to find Devonna, while Otischia, is at the ambulance with Martin.

The police evacuated the MGM and it is completely empty, not a sound, no bells going off, dead silence.

For The Sake of Love II

The police want to talk to Terri but she wants to get to Kamal and Martin, "I need to see my husband and my son."

The police are persistent, "We need to ask you some more questions, ma'am"

Terri can't think straight, "Excuse me, my name is Terri Dozier and if you don't know who I am, google me. I can't sit and answer questions when my husband and son have been shot."

The police officer looks at Terri and shakes his head, "Ma'am we don't care what your name is, we're trying to get to the bottom of what is going on."

The news media show up, and now it's a frenzy.

Terri's nervous, she doesn't want her face all over the news but it's too late,

In Ohio,

Breaking News,

"Coming to you live from the MGM in Maryland, Heiress Terri Dozier was kidnapped by a man we know only as Robert, her husband Kamal Bodkins and son, Martin Phillips Jr, shot by police, we will bring you updates as they happen."

Auntie Pam sees the news and immediately starts making phone calls.

Delores sees the news and is glued to the television, "oh my God, I need to get to Terri."

DeeDee sees the news, "hmmm, what's up with that?"

Mr. Phillips is in Washington DC and he makes calls to check on Martin.

Nina finally sees Devonna, "Devonna, oh my God are you alright!" she grabs Devonna and hugs her.

Devonna is hysterical, "he was going to kill us, Terri saved my life, she saved my life, Nina."

"Calm down, what happened, how did he get you?"

"I recognized him and I pulled out my phone to call you and Nina and he put a gun to me and made me walk with him to his room, I saw Terri, tied up and gagged. He was talking crazy and, and Terri," she burst out crying. "Terri had sex with him so he wouldn't kill me."

Nina consoles Devonna, "I called JC and he's on his way, he's using Terri's private plane."

"Terri got him a private plane?"

"Yes, that's your husband, you see that's who she really is."

"She saved my life, he was going to kill us, I just know it."

A paramedic walks over to the police, "One of the injured died, he lost a lot of blood and we couldn't save him."

Nina jumps up, "wait right here," Nina walks over to the paramedic, which one died."

"Excuse me ma'am who are you?"

Nina is breathing heavily, "I'm a close friend, who did?"

Nina hears someone scream, "Oh no, no, no," she runs to Terri.

Chapter Eleven

For the Sake of Love

Nina just overheard the paramedic say one of the injured died and now she's hearing screams coming from where Terri is. Nina walks away from Devonna and rushes over to her best friend.

As Nina approaches Terri she sees her and Otischia hugging, "Oh no it must be Martin."

"What's wrong, what's going on, "asks Nina.

Terri is hysterical, "they said one of the injured died on the way to the hospital and we don't know which one it is."

"Let's go to the hospital and find out," says Nina.

Terri can't pull herself together, "I need to put some clothes on, I can't go down there like this."

Otishcia goes back to Terri's room and grabs a pair of jeans and a blouse for her to wear to the hospital.

A black female police officer walks over to Terri, "Ms., we need you to come with us to the police station."

"For what, I need to get to the hospital and check on my son and husband."

The police officer changes her tone, "I'm not asking you I'm telling you to come with me."

Terri changes her tone also, "and I'm saying hell no."

"If you don't come with me, I'm, going to place you under arrest."

Terri looks at the officer and shakes her head, "another house nigga wilding her authority to the field niggas."

Nina and Otishcia can't believe Terri said that neither of them has ever heard her talk this way.

"I'm doing my job, ma'am"

"If you were really doing your job, then you would have told someone that this lady has spent the past 24 hours being held in a room with a lunatic, and she needs to check on her family," Terri dismisses the officer, "can someone call me a taxi, please"

The officer is annoyed and done with Terri's rich attitude, "Ma'am, I can take you in a police car now."

Terri looks at her and shakes her head no "I was born in 1966, not 66 hours ago,"

A white male sergeant walks up during the commotion, "Is this the lady that was being held, hostage."

Terri speaks up, "Yes, it's me."

"Ma'am, we're going to need to ask you some questions later, but first, I'm going to have a car take you to the hospital to be with your family."

"Is my husband okay? Is my son okay?"

"Ma'am, please go with this officer. She will take you to the hospital," the officer says without answering.

"I'm not riding with her; she wants to take me to a holding cell and interrogate me; I'm the victim!"

"No one is going to interrogate you, and I can assure you, you are not going to prison."

Terri grabs her sunglasses out of her purse, "I need to go out of another entrance."

The sergeant wants to know why: "Who are you hiding from."

"Do you know who this lady is," asked Nina.

"No," says the sergeant.

"This is Terri Dozier, does that ring a bell."

"No, I'm afraid not. Is she a rapper or a dancer?"

Nina's mind went crazy, and just as she was about to curse the sergeant out, Terri cut her off.

"No, I'm not a rapper or a dancer. However, I am the owner of the Cleveland Browns, Dozier marketing, Dozier cosmetics, and the list goes on."

The African American female officer stands down; she has no idea who Terri is.

The sergeant has a stupid look on his face, "ma'am, I'm sorry if I offended you."

"You didn't, but I understand your kind doesn't get out much."

The officer chuckles.

Terri turns to her, "You don't either, sista." Terri has had enough; now that everyone knows who she is, she wants to get to the hospital.

The sergeant takes Terri to a secret entrance that other famous people use to enter the MGM. She and Nina are then driven to the hospital in a police car with a siren on. On the way to the hospital, Terri realizes she doesn't have a cell phone because Rob took her phone and tossed it in the trash so no one would track her.

They pull up at the hospital and are taken to the morgue. Terri is terrified, "Why are we going here."

"We need you to identify the body."

"No, I can't do this," says Terri.

"I'll go in," says Otishcia. Otishcia is led into the morgue by the police.

The officer, along with the coroner, pulls out the body.

Terri turned around and faced the wall; she started praying.

Otishcia takes a deep breath when they remove the sheet from over the body; she lets out a sign once she sees who it is. She looks at the officer, "It's Rob."

Otischia is escorted back out to where Terri is, "Terri, is not Martin or Kamal; it's Rob; Rob is dead."

"Thank you, Jesus. Can someone please take me to my family?"

"Terri, before we see Martin and Kamal, there is something I need to tell you, but you have to promise not to say a word."

"Otishcia, what is it?"

For The Sake of Love II

Otishcia hesitates for a minute.

"Tish, tell me!'

"Your sister and Mrs. Phillips are responsible for your car accident, killing Chauncey and shooting me. They were trying to silence everyone who knew about Martin Jr. because she didn't want her husband to know, but the truth is he always knew and didn't say anything."

Terri can't move, this was a blow she was not ready for, "My sister tried to kill my family. She is a monster."

"Terri, remember you can't say anything; Martin does not want you to know."

"Ladies, let's move it to the emergency room," says the police.

Terri and Otischia are taken to the emergency room.

When Terri sees Kamal, she runs to him and says, 'Baby, baby, I'm so glad you're alright. I love you so much,' hugging him.

Kamal has a gunshot to his leg, and he's a little groggy from the pain medicine, "I'm fine; they were able to remove the bullet, but are you alright? Did he hurt you?"

"I'm fine, don't worry about me."

"Terri, did he hurt you? Tell me the truth!"

"Babe, he's dead, there's no need to worry about what he did, he's dead, and he can't hurt you again, and he told me that you are not the father of Tracie's baby, that Renee set it all up."

"Thank God, we are done with him," Kamal becomes emotional, "I love you; I would do anything to protect you."

"I know, I know, and I would do the same."

"Is Martin okay? I had no idea he had a gun. I showed him my gun, but he never showed me his."

"I need to go and check on my son; I'll be right back."

"Okay," Kamal tries to smile, "I'll be right here."

Terri runs to Martin's room, where she sees him and Otishcia embracing. She walks into the room and says, " Hey, handsome."

"Hi, Mom, are you okay?"

"Don't worry about me; I'm a tough cookie from the streets of Ohio; I'm good."

Otishcia looks at Terri, "really."

Terri winks her eye at Otishcia; yes, really.

"I am sore and ready to leave this place. Thank God I was wearing a bulletproof vest."

"You were," asked Terri

"Yep, I was ready for whatever was going to go down; all I knew was Rob was going to die."

For The Sake of Love II

"I guess you heard he's dead."

"Yep, and rightfully so, ain't nobody fucking with my family anymore and getting away with it," says Martin

"I feel the same way, son, I'm not letting anyone fuck with my family either, and I don't care who it is."

When they return from DC, they hear Renee is on the warpath about her husband, and Tracie is right along with her.

Tracie shows up at the vet hospital to see Kamal. " Excuse me, is Dr. Bodkin here?" Tracie rubs her stomach.

The Dr. is not here and won't be back for a few weeks," says the receptionist.

Kamal walks into the hospital and sees Tracie at the front desk. He is still a little weak from the gun shot.

"Tracie, what are you doing here," you shouldn't be here," says Kamal.

"You killed my father," she reaches inside her purse and pulls out a gun," so I'm going to kill you."

Everyone in the lobby runs out, and Kamal is standing alone, staring down the barrel of a thirty-eight. Kamal speaks calmly, "Wait, Tracie, you don't want to do this. You and I are having a baby."

"Nigga please, this is not your baby, I only fucked you to get back at your wife, and I lied; this is not your baby."

"Oh, okay, but I didn't kill your father, I swear to you."

Tracie clicks the gun, "Somebody is going to pay for my daddy's death, and it's going to be you."

Kamal is pleading with her and scared to death at the same time.

They hear the police sirens,

"Tracie, that's the police; you don't want to have your baby in prison, do you? If you put down the gun, I promise to tell the police it was a big misunderstanding and I won't press charges against you."

Tracie starts to cry, and her arm is getting heavy, holding the gun pointed at Kamal, "Who's going to pay for my father dying? You think because your wife has money, you can get away with murder."

"Tracie, my wife and I can give you money, and you and your baby can go and live well; just put the gun down."

The police negotiators start talking to Tracie and convincing her to let Kamal go.

After a twenty-minute standoff, Tracie decides to put the gun down, and the police rush in.

When the police handcuff Tracie, she turns around and looks at Kamal. " Are you still going to give us the money?"

"No, get her ass out of here."

Kamal tries to calm his nerves before calling Terri and telling her about Tracie..

For The Sake of Love II

Three weeks later great news

Martin and Kamal were released from the doctor's care, and the charges against both of them were dropped. Martin Sr. and Auntie Pam made some phone calls and got all the charges dropped.

In the meantime, the kidnapping did make headlines, and Terri's face was all over TMZ, the blogs, and TikTok. If someone didn't know who Terri Dozier was, they do now.

JC was grateful to Terri for saving his wife's life, but he felt bad about telling Rob about the girl's trip. He admitted to barely knowing Rob. JC finds out that Rob befriended him to get to Terri.

Terri hasn't slept well since the ordeal; she's had sleepless nights, and when she does sleep, she has nightmares about what Rob did to her. She hasn't been able to tell Kamal that Rob raped her. She's become a recluse; she doesn't take any phone calls from anyone, including Nina. Terri has been journaling every day since she returned home.

Kamal isn't taking any more chances; he realizes he has a high-profile wife and needs to protect her and their children at all times.

Martin and Otishcia are at her OB-GYN appointment. Martin, can you believe it? I'm really pregnant; it's a miracle."

Martin is looking at the baby on the monitor, "We need a miracle right now."

Otishcia looks over at him, "Are you ready to be a father?"

"Yes, and I'm ready to be a husband, I don't want my baby to come into this world without us being married."

"You're going to have to move fast because your little girl is not going to stay small, long."

"It's a girl, we're having a girl." Otishcia is excited.

Martin doesn't look excited.

"What's wrong; did you want a boy."

"Just having a girl, oh my goodness, I don't want her to have a boyfriend."

The doctor and Otishcia laugh.

"We have a long time before that happens," says Otischia.

Martin has a dumb look on his face.

"Let's go home, call my parents and your parents, and tell our friends, "I'm so excited."

"I would rather tell them the wedding date and then about the baby," says Martin.

"Okay, let's go home and set the date"

Otischia wants to tell her family and friends.

The date is set, and the planning has begun.

Otishcia and Martin decide to get married right away, and everyone wants to know what the rush is, but they are both keeping the baby hush hush; they decided on a destination wedding in Dubai.

It's been two months since the ladies got back from the MGM. Nina scheduled lunch or dinner dates for them three times, but Terri declined the invite each time.

Otishcia, Devonna, and Nina meet for dinner. Nina is the last one to arrive. " Sorry I'm late, but I had a lot of work to do today." Nina sits down at the table.

"So, Terri's not coming," asks Otishcia.

"She's your mother-in-law; you haven't talked to her," asks Nina.

"No, I haven't, and neither has Martin; it's like she has shut everyone out of her life."

"Give her time; I'm telling you guys; she went through a lot; that man tortured her physically and mentally. I'm surprised she hasn't snapped," says Devonna

"She seemed fine after it happened," says Nina.

"Yeah, but when the shit sets in, and you start playing it over and over in your head, it can make you snap," says Devonna.

"How are you doing," asks Nina.

"I have my good days and my bad days, you know. The man said he was going to kill me, and he put the gun to my head."

"Damn, you never told us that," says Otishcia.

"Terri had to fuck him to keep him from killing me; I'm telling you; she saved my life." Devonna starts crying.

"Let's talk about something else," says Nina.

"In a few more weeks, I'll be married; I'll be Mrs. Phillips," Otishcia says, all smiles and oozing with excitement about her wedding.

"Do you think Terri is going to attend," asks Devonna.

"Of course, her son is getting married; she is not missing our wedding."

The ladies conversed, finished eating, and parted ways, back to their lives.

Terri hasn't been feeling well, and she fears the worst may have happened; she walks into her bedroom, takes a pregnancy test, and waits for the results.

After twenty minutes, she looks at the two pink lines and says, "Oh no, I'm pregnant." She hears Kamal.

"Terri, Terri, baby, where are you?"

Terri doesn't know where to hide the test; she puts it in her bra."

Kamal walks into the room Terri pretends to journal.

Kamal walks over and kisses her, "Hello beautiful," he has yellow roses for her.

Terri smiles, "they are beautiful, but you smell like a kennel."

"You don't say, let me get out of these clothes and you and I are going to dinner."

Terri reacts negatively, "No, I don't want to leave the house."

"Baby, come on, it's been months," he sits beside her.

"I know, but I'm not ready to let people see me; I loved it when no one knew who I was. Now everyone knows me, and I have no privacy."

Kamal stares at Terri.

"What, why are you looking at me like that?"

"I don't know, something looks different about you."

"Please, I'm the same ole Terri."

"There's nothing old about you, and you are a beautiful woman."

"That's nice of you to say, but I'm closer to old than I am young." Terri rolls over to the lounge.

Kamal starts kissing her and touching her butt and between her legs.

"Stop, Stop, don't touch me!"

Kamal stops, "I'm sorry, what's wrong? We haven't had sex since."

"Since I was kidnapped, Kamal, I'm in no mood to have sex; I don't feel sexy; this was traumatic for me."

"I know, I know, and I'm sorry. I need to be more understanding. Will you at least sleep in our bed tonight?"

Terri shakes her head, "No, I don't want to."

"Will you kiss the baby or cuddle with him? You haven't been with him either."

Terri is irritated, "Leave me alone, please."

Kamal is not letting up, "Terri call a therapist and talk to them since you won't talk to me."

"Okay, I will," Terri doesn't mean it she just wants him to leave her alone.

For The Sake of Love II

A holiday wedding

The holidays are in a few weeks, and Otischia's mother and father have planned a beautiful Christmas wedding for their daughter in Dubai.

Thanksgiving came and went for Terri; it was just another day for her to stay in her room. It was embarrassing for Kamal because he invited his family and friends over. He hoped Terri would join them, but she didn't.

It's a week before Christmas, and while everyone is in good spirits, Terri is quiet and reserved.

It's blistering cold, a typical Boston winter day, Martin comes into the house wearing a parka coat, boots, scarf, and hat. He hands his coat and scarf to the housekeeper and takes his boots off. "Where is my mother."

The housekeeper points to the steps, "where she's been the last few months."

Martin walks up the stairs and knocks on her door, "Mom,"

Terri is staring out the window at the snow, "yes, come in." she turns to look at Martin as he walks through the door.

Martin can barely see her because the lights are off and the blinds aren't open all the way. " Why are you still in here? Come downstairs and have some soup with me."

For The Sake of Love II

"I don't feel well."

"What's wrong, are you sick!"

"No, calm down. I'm just not feeling good mentally or physically."

Martin reaches for her hand to hold, and she grabs a hold of his hand.

"You never told me; did you get a chance to have a long talk with Chauncy?"

"No," Martin stutters, "we never talked, and we never will," he mumbles.

"Did you call your sisters and invite them?"

"No, I didn't."

"Martin you should invite all of your family to your wedding."

"Including my grandmother?"

Terri hesitated, "No, not her."

My father, my adopted father, is coming, and you'll be there; I'm good."

"Okay, will you be there?"

"Of course I will; I will not miss my oldest son's wedding to one of my best friends."

"I have something to tell you."

"What?"

"Tish is pregnant, and it's a girl."

Terri is excited for them, "that is wonderful."

"We thought she could get pregnant, you know, after the shooting; that bullet was meant for me."

"How do you know that," asks Terri.

"I don't know that for sure; look, let's talk about something else."

For The Sake of Love II

Two days before the wedding, everyone is packed and ready to go.

Martin and Kamal have resolved their issues, and Martin asked Kamal to be a groomsman and Mr. Phillips his best man. Mr. Phillips was honored and will be bringing a date along with his other children.

Kamal looks at Terri as she walks toward him from the bathroom. "You are gaining weight."

"I know, I can see that; that's all the laying around."

"But you haven't been eating; hmm, that's strange."

"No, it's not strange, it happens," Terri wants to skip to another subject. "I need to take care of some last-minute issues that came up at the company, and I can't ask Martin to do it because he's getting married."

"So what are you saying, you're not coming?"

"No, you know I'm not going to miss the wedding; I'm in it. I'm saying you and the baby go ahead of me, and I'll meet you there."

Kamal looks at Terri suspiciously.

"Kamal, don't do that."

"I know my wife, and I think she's up to something."

"Nope, I'm only up to business," Terri kisses him.

Kamal grabs her and brings her close to him, "My dick is hard."

"Oh really," Terri laughs.

"Yes, woman, I want some pussy, I want to make love to my wife."

"When I get to Dubai, be ready because it's on, you hear me," says Terri

"Okay, I'm going to hold you to that."

Christmas Eve

The wedding party left for Dubai, and Kamal took the baby and boarded the plane along with everyone else. Terri is the only one not on the plane; however, she is in the air.

Terri's plane touches down in Ohio at 5 p.m. She steps off the plane wearing a long-hooded white mink coat, white sunshades, white gloves, a white tunic dress with the word "faith" written down the middle of the dress, and a pair of tall white stiletto boots. She looked like an Angel in all white.

Her long locks are draped around her neck and bounced as she walked to her rental car, a white four-door Lincoln SUV.

The Wedding,

Terri shows up in Dubai on time to help Martin and Otishcia prepare for the wedding.

"I thought you weren't going to make it," says Martin.

Terri embraces him tightly and says, "There's no way I'm going to miss my son's wedding."

Everyone I love is here witnessing my wedding, I wish," Martin stops.

"I know, but Chauncey is in heaven smiling because his three children are together and getting to know each other, and Mrs. Phillips, well, she's probably in hell getting her just due."

"Martin shot Terri a surprised glance. 'Really?'"

Terri attempts to repair the situation but realizes she is being insensitive to Martin. "Let's not discuss that; she is wherever she is."

"She was good to me despite trying to have me killed."

Just as Terri was about to say something, Kamal walked in., and clapped his hands, "It's time. Are you ready to do this?"

"Yes, I'm ready," says Martin.

Terri leaves the room.

Martin's hands are sweaty, and Kamal can see that he is nervous.

Kamal walks closer to Martin, "I know we have had our differences, but I have your back, and I'm here if you need me."

Terri is escorted down the aisle and is seated next to her Auntie Pam

Martin walked down the aisle; he was nervous and handsome at the same time. Terri looked at him, and as hard as she tried to fight back the tears, she could not. "That's my son," she looked at her aunt.

"Yes and he is a fine young man.," says Aunt Pam

Next up was the bride's maid, and the groomsman, Kamal, walked in as the best man.

The bride's entrance music played, and everyone stood up; Otishcia was gorgeous, and her little belly was poking out, but she was still beautiful, and no one could tell she was older than Kamal by twelve years.

Kamal was emotional as his bride-to-be walked toward him, but when it came time for him to say his vows, he was strong, and everyone saw he loved her.

The reception was underway, and everyone was having a great time. Terri danced with Kamal and the baby, feeling that her life was perfect.

After the party, Terri sat alone on the hotel terrace. She wore a long dress and a head wrap. She sipped her glass of wine and thought about the past forty-eight hours of her life.

"Terri, please don't do this, DeeDee and I will leave you and your family alone and never bother you again."

"No, I tried that, but you two couldn't leave me alone. She steals my money and tries to kill me and my children, and you think I'm going to let her live."

"Mom, don't worry, she isn't going to do it," says DeeDee

"Bitch, shut the fuck up," Terri fires at DeeDee but she doesn't die right away,.

"Mommy, help me."

Delores hovers over DeeDee's body, crying, "My baby." She looks at Terri, "you'll never get away with this."

Terri laughs, "I'm the smart one; she's the dummy. I planned it all out."

Delores looks at DeeDee, she's dead.

Delores screams

Terri enjoys hearing her mother scream and beg for her. "Why are you afraid to die, woman? You lived a mean life, and now you don't want to go to hell, is that it?"

"Goodbye, Mother," Terri shoots her mother, but she's not dead. Delores is choking on her blood."

"Finish the job, you coward."

"Now, I forgive you."

For The Sake of Love II

Terri sets the scene for a murder-suicide and looks around to make sure there aren't any traces of her being there; she walks out to her car and drives herself to a private runway.

Kamal walked up, "I don't know what is on your mind, but I need you present and in the moment."

Terri smiles, "I'm present and enjoying the lovely life that awaits my family."

What about your mom and sister?"

"I'll let life take care of them." Terri relaxes in Kamal's arms—the two kiss.

Once they returned from Dubai, Terri was back to her old self; it was as if she had a new life to live; she was ready to put the kidnapping and the rape all behind her.

A week later.

Terri's phone is ringing non-stop at 2am.

"Babe, answer your phone it may be important," says Kamal

"I'm sleeping they can call back."

Kamal answers her phone, "hello."

"Hello, can I speak to Aunt Terri,"

"Hold on," he says as he hands Terri the phone. Something is wrong; your niece is crying."

Terri takes her phone, "Hello, Channel, Chaundra, what's going on."

"Auntie, it's Mom she's dead; the police just left. They found her body in a cottage on Lake Erie with a letter from Grandma. Grandma killed our mother."

"Oh no, Where is your grandmother?"

"We don't know."

"Wait, she wasn't," Terri stops. I'll be right there," Terri hangs up.

"What's going on?"

"My sister was found dead in a cottage."

"I'll go with you."

"No, you stay here with the baby; I'll fly down and take care of the girls."

Terri was on a flight within three hours and landed; she went straight to DeeDee's house to her nieces.

They run to hug her, "Aunt Terri, what will we do? We don't have anyone," says Chaundra.

"You have me and your brother. I will oversee the funeral, and you two can come to Boston with me and your brother."

"We have grandma, too," says Chanel

"Why do you say you have her," asks Terri.

"Because we don't know where she is."

"She killed your mother, so she's going to prison."

Chanel and Chaundra began to cry.

Terri pretended to give DeeDee a funeral for her niece's sake. Only a few people attended the funeral, and Terri made sure it was a closed casket because she had already had DeeDee cremated, and her ashes thrown into a river.

For The Sake of Love II

Two years later

After enduring a lengthy period of chaos and uncertainty, Terri and Kamal have finally embraced a sense of stability as they settle back into their everyday routine. Their recent purchase of a stunning nine bedroom house, with its inviting impression and spacious interiors, has brought a renewed sense of joy. The house features large windows that flood the rooms with natural light and a cozy backyard that whispers promises of future family gatherings and laughter.

As they prepare for the arrival of their new baby, the couple burst with excitement. They imagine transforming one of the sunny bedrooms into a nursery, with soft pastel colors, whimsical decals on the walls, and a crib surrounded by plush toys waiting to be cuddled. Each corner of their new home buzzes with possibilities as they dream of family moments—storytime by the fireplace, baby's first steps on the gleaming hardwood floors, and the sweet sounds of cooing filling the air. Their hearts are full as they look forward to creating a warm, nurturing environment that will be the backdrop for countless cherished memories.

Kamal looked into Terri's office and saw she still hadn't had housekeeping unpack all of her boxes.

"This office is a mess," he walks in and starts unpacking, and while unpacking, he sees her journal.

He gently shuts the door and then explores the pages of her journal; his disbelief grows with every word he reads.

Terri goes looking for Kamal and calls his name. "Kamal, honey, where are you?"

The words in her journal completely grip Kamal.

"Kamal, Kamal, where are you, honey?" Terri pushes the door to her office open. " What are you doing in here?"

He looks at her but can't say anything.

"What are you reading?"

He was speechless.

Terri walked over to him and saw that he was reading her journal. She snatched it from him and said, "Why are you reading my journal? It's private."

Kamal stares at her with a blank look.

Terri stares back at him. This time, she's speechless.

Her cell phone rings, and she answers to avoid Kamal, "Hello."

"I'm still alive; I told you you can't kill me."

Terri dropped her phone. "Oh my God," she's screaming inside her head.

"Who is it, who was that."

"No one, no one." Terri was shaking.

Kamal stared at his wife, unsure of who or what he was married to.

For The Sake of Love II

THE END

For The Sake of Love II

Is Delores still ALIVE?